GLUNDA THE VEG WITCH

KEITH W. DICKINSON

HAMMERSMYTH PRESS

PROLOGUE

Alar Reave stumbled through the darkness, cursing anything and everything in sight. What the hell was he doing up at this ungodly hour? He should have still been in bed where it was nice and warm (if a little lonely). He pulled his cloak tight around him. God how he hated the winter. It had only just begun and already it was bitterly cold. What would it be like when the snows came? Pure misery, that's what.

Reluctantly, he popped a couple of slices of dried banana in his mouth, sucking on their energy to generate a field of warmth around him. He hated wasting some of his precious dried fruit on something so frivolous, but he hated the cold even more. He visualised his shelves at home, annoyed at how little dried fruit he had left. Pretty soon he'd be onto the jams and jellies, eking them out over the coming months until he could lay in some fresh supplies. That was the worst thing about winter. Not just the cold, but the fact that you had to rely on preserves to keep your magic alive. It wasn't just annoying, it was humiliating, and the worst part of it was, there was nothing you could do about it.

Crunching his way up the gravel path, he arrived at a farmhouse door. Resisting the urge to bang on it like a madman, he knocked twice and waited. Wurst may have been a terrible farmer, and not the brightest man around, but he was still a farmer, and any Drupe Mage caught disrespecting a member of that venerable profession would find himself out of fruit before you could say, "You call that a melon?!"

The farm door burst open. "Lord Reave! Come in, come in. May I take your cloak?" Wurst the Farmer, so brimming with excitement he'd buttoned his shirt up wrong, ushered the mage into his home.

"No. Just show me why you have summoned me here," said Alar Reave, ducking under the low doorway. "If you would be so kind," he added with a forced smile.

"Of course, my lord, of course. Please, right this way."

Wurst led the mage through the house and along a dark corridor towards a heavy black curtain. As they walked, Alar Reave felt the air get warmer. "You keep a cosy home, Master Wurst," he said, pushing his cloak back off his shoulders.

"Just you wait," said Wurst with a proud grin. He pulled the black curtain aside and a wave of hot air hit them. It took Alar Reave by surprise. The air was moist, too, and dank. Not to mention a little bit earthy. The only way Alar Reave could think to describe it was *fecund*.

They stepped into a small room made entirely of glass, lit by a dozen oil lamps. It should have been freezing in there, considering the weather outside, but Wurst had placed a couple of braziers either side of the doorway which produced a low, consistent heat that permeated the entire room. There were benches along each wall, covered in pots, and soil, and a variety of seeds, and a smattering of tools all about the place.

In the centre of the room sat a small tree in a large clay pot, barely more than a sapling; lush, green, and brimming with life.

"What's this?" whispered Alar Reave, barely able to believe his eyes.

"'Tis a tree, my lord," said Wurst proudly.

Alar Reave stepped forward. He touched the tree with great reverence. "But how did you make it so... green?"

Wurst shrugged. "'Tis just a question of having the right conditions, my lord. Once you can do that, you can do anything."

"And will it... fruit, do you think? Given the right conditions?"

With a grin, Wurst beckoned the mage round the other side of the tree. There, in all its glory, hung a single, glorious, juicy, golden pear. Alar Reave cried out in astonishment.

"Would you like to be the first to try it, my lord?" Wurst gestured towards the fruit. Alar Reave nodded dumbly. Reaching out a trembling hand, he plucked the pear from its branch, feeling its power as he took a hesitant bite. Its juices ran down his chin as he pierced its soft, golden flesh.

Immediately, he felt the magic course through him, the pear's energy welling up inside as he swallowed its sweet nectar. A dozen spells sprung to mind, spells he wouldn't attempt on dried fruit, never mind preserves. He felt like he could do anything, like he was in the full flush of the Spring Rush. Quite simply, he felt invincible.

"Is it good, my lord? Do you approve, sir?"

Alar Reave smiled at his new best friend. "Yes, Master Wurst. It is good. It is very good indeed."

Alar Reave gazed up at the tree, barely able to comprehend what such a discovery might mean. Fresh fruit all winter long. The Drupe Mages no longer having to rely on dried fruit and preserves to get by. It would change their lives. It would change the world. It would change everything!

Those damn Veg Witches didn't stand a chance.

CHAPTER ONE

G lunda knew it was unseemly for a witch to be giddy with excitement but she couldn't help herself; today was a big day.

She'd been pottering around her little witchy hovel all morning trying to keep busy (By tradition, all witches lived in 'hovels' although truth be told the word 'cottage' or 'house' might have been more appropriate.) She'd washed the dishes, swept the floor, scrubbed the tiles, and polished the door. She'd put on a stew, cleaned the conservatory, fed the spratty nibblers by letting them eat away at the dead skin on her feet, and she'd brought in buckets of water and chopped a load of wood for the sauna later. She was looking forward to the sauna, but not as much as she was looking forward to the stew. It was Change Day, so she hadn't had to be stingy. She'd thrown every last bendy bit of veg she had left into the pot. This time tomorrow her cupboards would be brimming with fresh potatoes, carrots, onions, and leeks. What did it matter if today they all stood bare?

The clock on the mantle chimed ten and Glunda clasped her hands together with glee. Finally, it was time to go!

Glunda already had on her blackest dress, and her finest red and black stripey socks. To this she added her best black lace shawl, and the new black pointy hat she had bought just for the occasion. It had been expensive, but it was worth it. After all, it wasn't every day one became Keeper of the Cauldron, the highest honour in all of witchdom.

In the parlour, Glunda put on her best worst boots. They were old and scuffed and practically falling apart but she wouldn't have changed them for the world. A witch's boots told the story of her life. They showed how she travelled o'er hill and dale, in good times and in bad, ministering to the sick, the elderly, and the permanently confused. They showed you where she'd been, where she was going, and what kind of a witch she would be when she got there. And, most importantly, they were proof that said witch was not someone to be trifled with. She was to be listened to, and obeyed, and yes sometimes even feared, because her wisdom was hard earned and her wrath swift and mighty. They would have to be, for her to have lived in such boots for so many a year. No one trusted a witch in brand new boots, and rightly so as far as Glunda was concerned.

Glunda opened her front door to find a small box of vegetables on her doormat. There was a note attached which read, 'Best of luck on your big day, Mistress. We're all very proud.' The note was from Mrs Brumley, the potato farmer's wife. She always was a wily one. She'd be round later with a proper tribute, once the ceremony was complete, but a gift like this was just the kind of thing to make you stick in a witch's mind. It meant that when spring came around and it was time for the witches to do their Favours, you would be first in line. Or, at the very least, that you wouldn't be last. The Granting of Favours was a subtle and complicated process after all. There were other things to take into consideration besides who had been fastest to your door.

Depositing the first of what would be many, many veggies to come on the dresser by the front door, Glunda set off for the Mage's Castle.

Viewed from the wooded copse atop a small rise that Glunda called home, the seat of the mages was just a stone's throw away, but getting there on foot was another matter. The road to the castle was not the most direct path. Hemmed in by hedgerows and boundary stones lain down over decades of intermarriage and dodgy dealings, it wound its way between the interlocking parcels of land like a drunk snake that had lost its way. More than once it doubled back on itself completely, and whilst following the meandering byway could be more than a little frustrating, especially when you were in a hurry, it was infinitely better than trying to negotiate with the local landowners to get the damn thing moved. Glunda had tried, once, when she was young and foolish (not so long ago). Never again!

Glunda waved to the men at work in the fields, bringing in the last of that autumn's harvest. The men waved back, their strained smiles fixed upon their grubby faces until the passing witch was well out of sight. She saw Farmer Miggins and his son trundling down the road towards her, their cart piled high with an impressive array of turnips.

"Farmer Miggins, hello! How lovely to see you."

The farmer doffed his cap. "And you, Mistress Ashwillow. On your way to see the mages, are we?"

"We are. It's the equinox, you know. Time for the witches to take charge once more."

"Aye, so it is, so it is." Farmer Miggins spat over the side of his cart.

"I'll be by later to see about the Offering, if that's alright? You'll be in, I suppose?"

"Can't imagine I'll be anywhere else," said Farmer Miggins, a strange look in his eye.

"Excellent, excellent. Well, don't let me keep you. You must be very busy. I'll see you this afternoon. Goodbye, Farmer Miggins. Goodbye, Clum." The farmer's son gave her a half wave as he studiously avoided eye contact.

Glunda set off down the road, Farmer Miggins watching her go out the corner of his eye. "Aye, we'll be seeing you alright," he growled, elbowing his son in the ribs. "What do you say, lad? Reckon she'll like the Offerin' when she comes?"

"I dunno, Dad," mumbled his son, eyes firmly fixed upon the ground. His father laughed and cracked his whip, sending their cart lurching off down the road.

According to her father's watch, Glunda arrived at the Mage's Castle a full half an hour before the handing-over ceremony was due to begin. In her excitement she must have been walking awfully fast. Sitting down on a large rock by the side of the road, she chewed on a carrot whilst she waited for the world to turn a little further. She didn't want to arrive too soon otherwise she might have to make small talk with the mages, the very idea of which filled Glunda with stomach-churning dread and disdain.

She wished that some of the other witches had come along with her, for moral support. Once upon a time they would have, the handing-over ceremony being an important and solemn occasion worthy of recognition, but it had happened so many times over the years — once during the spring equinox when the mages took control of the land, and once during the autumnal equinox when the witches took it back — that no one seemed to care anymore. There used to be music, and speeches, and people cheering. Now you just turned up, took back the Golden Key, and that was it, job done. Glunda had asked once why they used a gold key to symbolise lordship over All That Can Be Surveyed, but the only response she'd ever gotten was a very grumpy, "Away wid ya!" along with the threat of a clip round the ear, so she'd decided to let that one go, for now. Some questions, it seemed, weren't meant to be answered (like why they called it a lordship when for six months of the year the people in charge were quite clearly of the lady variety).

Glunda found it strange that all the mages in the land chose to live right on top of one another in one big castle. It must be very noisy, and smelly, and full of... stuff. How was someone ever meant to get a proper night's sleep? But they seemed to like their big, red-brick monstrosity, so much so in fact that barely any mages had been seen outside its high walls all summer. You normally got one or two wandering about the place, but this past six months they'd all been secreted away from the world working on something big. Or that was the rumour at least. Large shipments of wood and glass had been seen heading through the castle gates, and there had been all kinds of banging and shouting and strange orange lights at night that no one could explain. Not that it really mattered, of course. Whatever the mages got up to in there was of no concern to Glunda. So long as they stayed out of the way and didn't interfere with her coming lordship (they really needed a better name for that) they could bang away to their heart's content for all she cared.

Glunda considered another carrot. It was always good to have a little magic to hand when dealing with mages, but she decided against it. One would be enough to keep her safe should anything untoward happen. Checking her father's watch once more, Glunda made her way up to the castle's huge double doors.

In the circular throne room at the centre of the big red castle, Alar Reave stood talking to Cheeves, the castle's burly Major Domo. "Bring her straight here when she arrives, and re-member, don't answer any of her questions. I'll deal with—"

CLANG! CLANG! CLANG!

A loud knock resonated throughout the castle. Alar Reave smiled. The witch must have used her magic to knock that loudly. She can't have appreciated finding their front door closed to her. Shame really, as it was something she was going to have to get used to.

"It appears our guest has arrived," said Cheeves. "Shall I show her in, sir?"

Alar Reave peeled a banana with glee. "Oh indeed, Cheeves," he said between bites. "Please, show her in. Show her in at once!"

By the time her knocks were finally answered, Glunda was absolutely fuming. "Took you long enough! Why is this door closed? Didn't you know I was coming?"

The Major Domo raised a solitary eyebrow. "We consider it prudent to keep our doors and windows closed at all times, madam. How else is one meant to keep the burglars at bay?"

"Ha! Burglars indeed. A witch's door is never locked. We've nothing to fear from thieves and the like, let me tell you!"

The Major Domo swallowed a comment about having nothing worth stealing as he smiled his most professional smile. "If you would follow me, mad—" he began, but Glunda had already barged her way past him.

Glunda marched across the castle courtyard. She didn't know where she was going, but she was too embarrassed to stop now. She'd let her anger get the better of her, something a witch should never do. She wasn't going to compound that mistake by stopping to ask for directions. Up some steps and through an open wooden door, she found herself in a long hallway. Slowing her walk so she could inspect the many tapestries that hung on the walls — lots of mages striking dramatic poses as they summoned things or vanquished things, usually atop hills or on open fields of battle, but always with some kind of wind coming from somewhere judging by the flap of their robes and the heroic wave of their flowing, manly locks — Glunda allowed the mage's servant to catch up with her.

The Major Domo led Glunda down the long, carpeted corridor to a large set of double doors. Pushing them open, he stood in the opening and announced her arrival. "Glunda Ashwillow," he exclaimed. "Mistress of the West Riding, Keeper of the Sacred Oath, and Protector of the village of Wellety Vale."

At least he got that bit right, thought Glunda, as the Major Domo stepped to one side. She marched into the room only to pull up short a few paces in. A lone mage sat on a golden throne on the other side of the room, an arm thrown casually over the back of the chair, a big goofy smile on his annoyingly familiar face. He waved to Glunda across the far too empty hall. "Glunda! Welcome. Please, do come in."

Glunda stepped forward slowly. "Alar? What's going on? What are you doing here? Where's everyone else?"

The mage hopped off his seat and wandered towards her. "I asked if I could be the one to greet you, given our long history. I hope you don't mind?"

Ha! Long history indeed, thought Glunda. If pulling a girl's pigtails and running away could be called a long history then yes, they had it by the bucket load!

Glunda and Alar had been at school together. Being the only school for miles around, there hadn't been much choice. But that had been the full extent of their association. That and the hair pulling. Alar had moved with the popular crowd, always laughing and joking and never taking anything seriously, whilst Glunda had kept herself to herself, getting on with her work whilst she waited for the world to change in her favour. She used to see him out the window of the school library running about, always with a phalanx of pretty girls chasing after him. Alar Reave was handsome, and he knew it, and whilst she hated to admit it, Glunda knew it too. Not that it really mattered. Glunda was in no doubt about the type (and shape) of girl someone like Alar went for — slim of hip, humour, and intellectual capacity — and whilst she was certain they would have made a formidable pairing given the opportunity, she was undoubtedly a little too well-rounded for the likes of him.

There was also the question of money. Alar's parents were rich, meaning he was always destined to become a mage. Glunda's parents were... Glunda didn't know if there was a word for being poorer than poor, but if there was then they were it. She'd had to work hard to get where she was today, harder than Alar Reave, that's for sure, so to have to deal with him now, in her moment of triumph, left a bitter taste in her mouth. It also didn't make any sense.

The two met in the centre of the room. "Where is the Guardian of the Golden Key?" said Glunda. "Why is he not here?" She didn't know exactly what was going on, but she did know that Alar Reave was most certainly not the man in charge.

"Lord Lansome is... around. I was hoping we could catch up first."

Glunda blinked several times. "But what about the ceremony?"

"All in good time. First, I must say, well done you! Keeper of the Cauldron and still so young. Very impressive. Tell me, do they give you a big wooden spoon to stir it with or do you have to provide your own?"

Glunda frowned. "Spoon? I don't… There's no actual cauldron, y'know. It's just a title."

"Ah! Of course, of course. Silly me. But even so, for someone our age to be given such great responsibility. The other witches must think very highly of you?"

"I suppose they do," said Glunda, looking around the room. "Look, I'm sorry, but where is the key? Is it here? Could we get it, do you think? Only I'd like to be getting on."

"Absolutely we can!" said Alar Reave. "I tell you what, why don't you follow me and we can see what's to be done about this key of ours, eh?"

Alar headed through a small door at the back of the room. After a moment's hesitation, Glunda followed him out.

Alar led Glunda down a long corridor that was clearly only meant for the use of servants. Several other corridors led off from it down which various soapy smells and culinary clangs and clatters could be heard. She was about to protest the indignation — Glunda wasn't precious about her surroundings, you understand. She would happily enter the filthiest of homes to minister to the sick and dying should the need arise, she just preferred for it to be of her own choosing and not somebody else's — when the corridor came to an abrupt end at another unimpressive small wooden door.

Pausing long enough to toss Glunda a quick cheeky wink, Reave pushed open the door.

The inner courtyard of the mage's castle was bright and warm and decidedly musty. Too musty in fact. Looking up,

Glunda saw what all the wood and glass had been about. A frame, like the truss-work of a cathedral but a little less organised, had been built over the courtyard to keep the heat in and the weather out. It didn't look particularly safe, but it did seem to be doing the job. The courtyard air was warm and moist, like a forest after a heavy rain, perfect for the many rows of trees the mages had inexplicably decided to plant there.

The entire courtyard had had its paving slabs removed, and the soil beneath dug up, turned, aerated, and fertilised. It must have taken them weeks to do, as they would have had to do it by hand. There was no way they could have got a horse in there to plough it up for them. Rows of trees had been planted to form a tightly packed orchard, with a few banana plants wandering about for good measure. Glunda saw mostly apples and plums and pears and satsumas, with a few pineapple and mango plants near the centre, where they would get the most light. She didn't know if that was by accident or design, and she wasn't about to ask.

"What do you think?" said Alar.

"I think you've made a mess of what used to be a perfectly lovely courtyard," said Glunda.

Alar laughed. "Yes. The architect would turn in his grave if he saw what we'd done to the place."

Glunda walked over to the nearest tree. She touched its trunk. It was real, and very fertile (she could feel it through the bark), with big juicy apples that looked very tempting indeed. But it was also not a happy tree. It was tired, and confused, and a little bit homesick. She got the impression that if it had been a guest as a party, it would have left hours ago, after standing in the kitchen all night feeling sorry for itself.

"What is going on, Alar? Why are you showing me this?"

Alar Reave plucked some fruit from the unhappy tree. "It's like this," he said, tossing the apple lightly in his hand. "My fellow mages and I have had enough of this whole handing a key back and forth business, so we've decided to hang on to it for a while."

Glunda's mouth went dry. "What do you mean?"

Alar Reave shrugged. "Just that," he said, "We're going to hang on to the key, and the stewardship, and everything else that entails, and you witches can go... well, go do whatever it is you do best, I suppose."

"But– But– You can't! What about the agreement? The land. The people. Who will take care of them?"

"We will, of course."

"But how can you? When winter comes—"

"When winter comes we will have a steady supply of fruit, as you can see. More than enough to deal with whatever minor problems or petty squabbles may arise. I mean, if you lot can do it..."

Alar Reave trailed off with a disinterested shrug. Fuming, Glunda drew herself up to her full height. "You won't get away with this," she said. "The people will not stand for it, do you hear? When they find out what you've done, they'll... they'll..." Glunda wasn't sure what the people would do, but she was sure it would be something unpleasant, possibly involving torches and pitchforks and the like.

Alar Reave smiled at her knowingly. "Oh, I think you'll find the people won't mind one bit," he said, taking a bite of his apple.

There's an old saying, 'bad news travels faster than a witch on the promise of a free meal', so it came as no surprise to Glunda to find her tiny hovel overrun by a gaggle of crotchety witches when she got home, all of whom had helped themselves to a bowl or two of her slow-cooked vegetable stew whilst they waited. What did surprise her was the fact that there was any stew left, not that she was about to get the chance to enjoy it. She'd barely got the door open before all the shouting began.

"Glunda! What happened? Where's the key?"

"Did they hurt ya at all, lassie?"

"I cannae believe they would do such a thing."

"I told you she were too young fer all this. Didn't I tell ya!"

"Now now, Mistress Oakenleaf. This is not her fault."

"Oh aye! An' whose fault is it, eh?"

"What'll they do when the fruit runs dry?"

"They must have something up their sleeves. A right wily lot these Drupe Mages, and no mistake!"

"It's not anyone's fault."

"I knew a Drupe Mage once, proper wily he was…"

"Yes, we *all* know how you knew 'im an' all, Viola Hawthorne."

"Oh, it's somebody's fault alright. You mark my words. *Somebody* is to blame."

"And what do you mean by that?! Ismay Silverbirch!"

"Has anyone got 'nymore of that lovely bread?"

Glunda pushed her front door closed wearily. "Mistresses, please. A moment if I may." She walked through the collected harangue of witches and plonked herself down on the only seat left available to her, a short wooden stool with a wonky leg by the fireplace.

A bowl of soup and a spoon appeared in her hand. "Take your time, lass," said Mistress Hearthcrow with a sympathetic smile. "Whenever you're ready."

The witches waited whilst Glunda took a few mouthfuls of soup. They might forget to respect the person now and then, but they never forgot to respect the earth's beauteous bounty.

"Right, are we gonna hear what 'appened?" barked Mistress Oakenleaf. "Or should we just break oot the beer an' call it a night?"

Mistress Hearthcrow sighed loudly. "Well, Glunda, what happened? Where's the Golden Key?"

Glunda told them what happened and, to their credit, the witches let her get most of it out before they started shouting again.

"So, it's glass hooses noo, is it!"

"Whoever heard of such a thing."

"Those poor trees."

"Is there no something we can dae?"

"What can we do? With all that fruit the Drupe Mages are too powerful. It would be war!"

"Aye, but if there was'nae inny fruit. Whit then?"

"Poison that land, you mean! Kill off all the trees."

"How awful!"

"I was thinking more like a few bricks o'er the castle walls, smash some windows, but aye, we could talk aboot a wee poisonin' if yer like."

"Is there more tea in the pot?"

Glunda listened glumly to the old witches bicker. They were very careful not to say it was all her fault, but they were also very careful not to say it wasn't all her fault either (Witches were always very careful about what they said in front of other witches. You never knew what off-hand comment would come back to bite you later in life.) She looked across at Mistress Hearthcrow, who was keeping well out of it. Witches didn't have a leader, you couldn't lead a bunch of witches any more than you could herd a group of cats, but if there had been one, Marleena Hearthcrow would have been it. She was wise, and caring, and stern when needed, but most important of all she knew when to keep quiet and when to speak, a skill most people knew nothing about (not in any meaningful way at least). She didn't bother talking over all the other voices clamouring for attention. She simply sat there sipping serenely at her tea whilst she waited for everyone else to run out of steam. Only when the other witches started to repeat themselves did she finally clear her throat to speak.

"Mistresses, I think perhaps now is not the time to resolve this matter. I suggest we reconvene in a few days' time. Let us see what we can find out, then we can decide how best to respond. Agreed?"

The gathered witches nodded their agreement, some with great reluctance. Mistress Oakenleaf was eyeing up the bricks in Glunda's hearth like she was curious about their aerodynamic properties. Taking a few moments to scrape the last from their bowls of stew, the witches headed out one by one, thanking Glunda for her hospitality as they shuffled out the door. Eventually only Mistress Hearthcrow remained.

"Get yourself some rest, Glunda," she said. "You've had a hard day. And don't worry, things will look better in the morning."

"You are most kind, Mistress Hearthcrow. I... I'm sorry I made such a mess of things. I don't know what happened."

"The Drupe Mages, that's what happened," said Mistress Hearthcrow. "This is clearly something they've been planning for a long time. It was just your bad luck you were the one they sprung it on. I doubt any of us would have reacted any different, no matter what Jemima Oakenleaf has to say on the matter." The witch donned her coat and hat. "You did the right thing walking away. No point getting yourself killed over some damn key." She headed for the door.

"Thank you, Mistress Hearthcrow. That's good of you to say."

Mistress Hearthcrow stopped in the doorway. "Key or no key, you are the Keeper of the Cauldron now, Glunda. You must call me Marleena."

"I will, Marleena. Thank you."

With a last reassuring smile, Mistress Hearthcrow left Glunda in a living room that now smelt faintly of lavender, moss, burnt sage, and gin, surrounded by a vast array of dirty cups, bowls, plates, and what looked like every piece of cutlery she owned. Glunda looked round at the mess, at the pot standing empty on the kitchen stove, and at the space on the mantle she had reserved for the Golden Key. Then, plonking herself down on the nearest chair, she buried her head in her hands and had herself a good old-fashioned unwitchy cry.

CHAPTER TWO

Clum Miggins sat at the kitchen table — in his hand-me-down clothes, with his hand-me-down haircut — jabbing listlessly at a bowl of porridge. His father burst in, whistling a jolly tune. Tossing a dead chicken next to his son's breakfast, he went to wash his bloody hands. "Mornin', son! How ya diddlin' on this fine mornin'?"

"Fine, I guess," said Clum, using the non-spoon end of his spoon to push the twitching bird carcass further away from him.

"That's my boy," said Clum's father, not really listening as usual. Clum's father had been in a good mood ever since their encounter with Mistress Ashwillow the day before. It was really starting to get on Clum's nerves. "Think we'll see our little witch today then?" his father said, gazing out the kitchen window.

"I 'spect," said Clum. "She's due her Offerin' after all, ain't she?"

"Well, we'll just see what she's due when she gets here, eh." His father winked at Clum.

"She did the work, Dad. She should get what's coming to her."

"Oh, don't you worry, son," his father said gleefully. "She'll get what's coming to her alright."

Glunda Ashwillow awoke face down on her bed, fully clothed. The sound of someone who enjoyed tidying up after people wafted in through her open bedroom door. With a sigh at what she knew she was about to find, Glunda dragged herself upright, brushed down her crinkled skirt, and clumped her way down the narrow hallway into the kitchen.

A young witch stood at Glunda's sink, scrubbing with grim determination at a pot that Glunda had given up on a long time ago. It was only still here because she hadn't bothered to throw it out yet. But the young witch wasn't to know that, so she'd set about cleaning it with such gusto that you could see the copper at the bottom of the pan again, and it was only a matter of time before you'd be able to see your face in said copper too.

Hearing a noise behind her, the young witch spun around, jangling as she turned. Whereas most witches opted for your basic black with no adornments for their day-to-day, Ellsa Puddleglump, the young witch from over the hill, had never found an outfit that couldn't be improved by adding something sparkling or musical (or both) to its folds and fringes. A lot of the older witches looked down on Ellsa for what they called her 'frivolous ways', but she got the job done, and she always left the world better than she found it, so as far as Glunda was concerned she could wear all the jingly jangly bits and bobs she liked.

"Oh! Glunda, I didn't hear you get up. I was just, um... Well, there was such a mess, so I thought I might... I mean..." Ellsa avoided Glunda's gaze. "I hope you don't mind?"

Glunda sighed a second time. Poor Ellsa. Who on Earth would mind someone else tidying their house up for them? "Of course I don't mind, Ellsa. Thank you." Glunda went over to fill the kettle, only to find it was already full and had just been brought to the boil, of course.

"I was going to make us something to eat but, um, I couldn't find anything. Did you not get your Offering?"

"I didn't, no. What with everything else that went on yesterday I guess I forgot."

"Yes, I heard about what happened at the castle." Ellsa didn't ask if Glunda was alright. That wasn't the done thing amongst witches. "Well anyway, I have my cart with me. We can go out after breakfast and get what you're owed if you like?"

Glunda smiled. Nothing warms the heart more than someone who is happy to help. "Thank you, Ellsa. That would be much appreciated."

Glunda and Ellsa trundled down the road in Ellsa's rickety old cart, the bench seat squeaking unhappily beneath their combined weight. Built for one, and smoother roads than this, it was earning its keep today.

Ellsa was something of a town witch, which was why she had her own cart. Towns were horrible places where people went to make their fortunes only to die in poverty. Everything cost so much in town, but people paid it willingly in the hopes of greater wealth in the future, all whilst living off other people's charity in the meantime. The greater part of Ellsa's time was spent carting food and clothing from those that had it to those in need, with the occasional transport of the sick and dying in between. A town witch could find many uses for a good sturdy cart, none of them particularly nice.

"My Offering was rather good this year. Of course most of it will go on soup for the poor, but still it's nice to know your work is appreciated."

"Indeed."

"I'm sure your villagers can't wait to show their appreciation of you, Glunda. Do you think the cart will be big enough for their Offering?"

Glunda glanced at the cart, which was long enough to lie down in, but barely wide enough to stretch out your arms.

"I'm sure it'll be fine. But if not we can always make two trips."

"Oh absolutely. Whatever you need," said Ellsa, grinning from ear to ear.

Bless her, thought Glunda. She's just happy to be here.

The cart turned down the dirt track that led to the Miggins's farm. Glunda saw Clum in the yard, looking like he'd lost a penny, then lost another penny during the search for the first one. "Hello, Clum. Is your father in? I've come to see about the Offering."

Clum looked uncomfortable. "He is, yeah." He left, giving the two witches a backward glance as he went.

"Nice lad," said Ellsa.

"I suppose," said Glunda.

"Much in the way of prospects?" said Ellsa casually.

Glunda knew exactly what she meant. "He's a bit more work than you're likely to get out of him. I doubt any woman of sense would take him on... Which probably means he'll be married by the end of the week around here."

Ellsa slumped slightly in her seat but said nothing.

Clum exited the farmhouse followed by his father. The elder man was smiling for once, which made for a nice change, but it set Glunda's senses a-tingling. It's a poor witch who can't spot when something is amiss.

"Ah, Glunda! Lovely to see you. Welcome to my humble home."

"Mistress Ashwillow, if you don't mind, Mr Miggins. I am Keeper of the Cauldron this year, after all."

The farmer's smile changed shape, but only slightly. "Farmer Miggins, if you don't mind, Mistress Ashwillow. I am keeper of these lands this year, and many years before that an' all."

"And a fine job you do of it too, Farmer Miggins. Speaking of which, I've come to see about this year's Offering. My apologies for not coming sooner. I was a little busier than expected yesterday."

"Yes, indeed," said Farmer Miggins with a twinkle in his eye. "Had a bit of fun at the old castle, I hear."

"Something like that," said Glunda. "But anyway, I can't stand around chatting all day. I have a great many people to see. So, if you don't mind..."

"Of course, of course. Wouldn't want to keep such an important person as yourself any longer than I 'as to. Please, come this way." Turning on heel, he walked off towards the barn.

"Good sir! Should we bring the cart as well?" Ellsa called out after him.

Farmer Miggins's smile changed once more. "Oh, I wouldn't worry about it. Between the two of you I think you'll be fine."

Farmer Miggins led Glunda through the barn, past boxes of freshly picked carrot and cauliflower to a small pile of misshapen vegetables best described as measly, or quite possibly meagre if you were feeling generous, but certainly not appetising in any way. If the barn had been a shop then it was five minutes before closing on a Saturday afternoon and this was all that was left.

Glunda regarded the knobbly crop of crass comestibles coldly. "You better be showing off your seedlings for next year," she said.

"Whatever do you mean?"

Glunda picked up an already wilting carrot. "What's this?"

"'Tis thy Offering, of course."

"It's an insult is what it is. What're you playing at, Miggins?"

Finally the farmer's smug smile fell away. "That's yer payment for last year's work. I didn't get half the spuds I were expecting to, and me runner beans were a right disaster. By my reckonin' that's what your work was worth."

"You'd have got a sight less if'n me and mine hadn't helped you out. And what about next year, eh? Is this meant to cover next year's Blessing an' all? Because I don't see how it will."

"Oh, don't worry about next year, Mistress. The mages have said they'll sort it for us."

"The mages! Are you kidding me? What do they know about gathering energy and keeping the land fertile? All they know is beer, bread, and blowing things up. They wouldn't know a ritual of fecundity if it came up and bit them on the—" Glunda caught Ellsa staring at her open mouthed. She took a deep breath. "Thank you, Farmer Miggins. I shall take my Offering and be on my way." Glunda waved for Ellsa to grab a box or two.

"If'n you need any more to see you through the winter I can sells you some... at a fair price."

"No thank you."

"You'll need to get in quick, mind. Coz this lot'll be going to market soon."

"I understand. Thank you."

Farmer Miggins shrugged. "Well, if'n you change your mind let me know. Always happy to help out our local witch, after all. Ain't that right, Clum?"

Clum stared resolutely at his own feet. "Yes, Dad," he mumbled reluctantly.

Glunda and Ellsa sat in silence as their cart trundled down the narrow country road, a sorry array of vegetables rolling about in the cart's bed behind them. The unpleasantness that had occurred at the Miggins's farm had happened at all the rest, more or less, although Farmer Miggins was the only one to take outright pleasure in Glunda's humiliation. They'd tried to explain it away with talk of bad weather, poor harvests, and high prices for shoddy goods that they just couldn't say no to, but it all amounted to the same thing; a middle finger to Glunda, and all she stood for, and barely enough vegetables to see her through 'til next spring.

The only farms who had honoured their agreement in full were the ones where the wives held sway, the women folk being too decent (or too canny) to insult a witch so openly. Even young Clum had felt ashamed enough by what his father had done to slip Glunda an extra sack of potatoes when his father wasn't looking. For a boy who grew up without a mother he was a good lad right enough.

Glunda caught Ellsa glancing at her out the corner of her eye. She clearly had something to say, but Glunda wasn't in the mood to make it easy on her by asking what it was. A witch needed to be forceful, to speak up, to say what was on her mind. Any witch who couldn't do that, couldn't stand up for herself, was no kind of witch at all (an irony that was not lost on Glunda).

"Glunda? What happened yesterday? With the mages, I mean."

It was a fair question. If only Glunda had a reasonable answer. "They refused to give up the key, Ellsa. They've built themselves a glass house to keep their trees warm, so they can have fresh fruit all winter. They think this means they don't need us, that they can do everything themselves, so they refused to give up the key."

"But... but that doesn't make any sense. What about us? What about the agreement? Who's in charge now?"

"For the moment they are. There's nothing we can do, unless we go to war." Ellsa looked horrified at the idea. "But I wouldn't worry about it if I was you," said Glunda. "They're bound to come a cropper soon enough, then we'll see who's in charge of what around here."

Ellsa smiled at Glunda's reassuring words, although as smiles go, it wasn't a very confident one.

⁂

At Glunda's request, Ellsa dropped her off at Mistress Hearthcrow's house. Their conversation had started the wheels turning, and she wanted to run some ideas past her whilst they were still fresh in her mind.

"I'll put your veg into storage for you," said Ellsa.

"Thank you, Ellsa, but you don't have to do that. On the kitchen table will do fine."

"Oh no, it'd be my pleasure. Besides, it won't take me very... long." Ellsa's voice trailed off as she caught sight of the sorry pile of vegetables.

"Yes, well, thank you for your help today, Mistress Puddleglump. I'm sure I owe you a cream tea or something."

Ellsa gave an uncertain smile. "Oh, um, not at all... Mistress Ashwillow. Any time."

Glunda knocked on Mistress Hearthcrow's front door. The senior witch had a nice house, befitting of her status; a two-storey cottage with a newly-thatched roof, roses around the door, and a sizeable vegetable patch tended once a week by one of the local lads. It was the sort of a place you got by knowing who was who, what was what, and who to give what to when, when the time came.

The front door swung open. "Ah, Glunda! Perfect timing. Do come in."

Glunda noticed a broomstick leaning against the wall by the front door. Like a lot of witches her age, Glunda saw a flying broomstick as an extravagant waste of magic. They were still popular amongst the older witches though, who saw history and tradition as far more important than they probably should be. "You have company, Mistress Hearthcrow?"

"I do, Glunda. Mistress Oakenleaf. She has come to… voice her opinion." The senior witch leaned close to Glunda's ear. "Truth be told, I'm glad you're here. She's a bit fired-up over this key nonsense. Perhaps between the two of us we can calm her down a bit." She straightened up again. "And I've told you before, call me Marleena."

Glunda chuckled. This first name thing would take some getting used to, but get used to it she must. She was second to no one now.

In the living room, Jemima Oakenleaf was pacing the floor, a 'medicinal' drink in hand. "There she is. Oor eshteemed leader. Maybe now we can start gettin' somewhere." It seemed that rather a lot of medicine had been consumed already that day.

"And a good afternoon to you too, Mistress Oakenleaf. Tell me, what seems to be the problem?"

"Seems? Don't give me 'seems', lass. You know what the problem is."

"Less of the lass, Jemima Oakenleaf," said Mistress Hearthcrow. "That's the Keeper of the Cauldron you're addressing, not some young witch fresh off the turnip wagon."

"Even without the key?" said Mistress Oakenleaf, reaching for the nearby bottle.

"*Especially* without the key," said Mistress Hearthcrow, deftly whipping the bottle out of reach.

"Is that what's got you fired up, Jemima? This whole key nonsense," said Glunda.

The other witch eyed Glunda furiously. It was the first time she'd ever used her given name. "Aye, it is. What d'ya propose to do about it, *Glunda*?"

Glunda shrugged. "I propose to do nothing. I think the mages have made a terrible mistake. I don't think they've thought about how challenging a long hard winter can be. Or how much work it is keeping everybody alive and satisfied. Once they do, they'll be begging us to take charge again, I'm sure."

"So that's yer plan, is it? Tae sit around waitin' fer things tae get better?"

"What would you have me do?"

"Have at 'em! Give 'em what for! Show 'em we ain't to be trifled with."

"War, you mean?"

"Aye, lass, war."

"A war would not benefit anyone," said Mistress Hearthcrow. "People die and nobody wins, not in the long run."

"Well, it'd make me feel a lot better," mumbled Jemima Oakenleaf.

"No, I think Glunda is right. Wait it out, see how it goes. The mages will mess up soon enough, then we'll have them right where we want them."

Mistress Oakenleaf climbed unsteadily to her feet and grabbed her bottle of medicine. "Aye well, you sit around waitin' if yer like, but I ain't waitin' for no Drupe Mage to decide *my* fate."

"Please don't do anything rash," said Glunda. "We don't need any trouble right now."

"Trouble is upon us, lassie, whether ye like it or not!"

Jemima Oakenleaf stumbled from the room. They heard the front door slam, and a mumbled incantation as she got her broom in the air. There was a woody clatter as she clipped the top of a tall tree, then a glassy smash as her bottle hit the ground below, the departing witch lamenting the loss of her lethal libation as only a native of the frozen north ever could, with language that would make a docker's toes curl.

"That went better than I thought it would," said Marleena Hearthcrow from over by the window. "Although I doubt my strawberries will ever be the same again."

"She seemed awful fired up," said Glunda. "Do you think I've done the right thing?"

"Indeed I do," said Mistress Hearthcrow. "Don't listen to Jemima. She's never met an opportunity for restraint she wouldn't gleefully ignore. Now is not the time to rush in. We need to see how things develop before making any absolute decisions."

Glunda played nervously with one of the tassels on her dress. "How was your Offering this year, Marleena? Did you get all that was coming to you?"

"I did, yes. More or less. There were a few who tried to shortchange me, there always is, but I just reminded them of what a bad idea that would be and they soon saw sense. Why? How did your Offering go?"

"Not so well, I'm afraid. Most came up short, with at least one being rather unpleasant about the whole thing."

Mistress Hearthcrow poured Glunda a cup of tea. "Yes, I can imagine some have felt emboldened by what the mages have done. It's annoying, but there it is I suppose. Not to worry though. They too will come to their senses once spring comes around."

She passed Glunda her tea, smiling. Glunda smiled back briefly. It was all well and good saying not to worry when you had a store full of vegetables. She wasn't the one who had to figure out how to survive until the spring thaw came.

Glunda sipped her tea in silence, a newfound appreciation for Jemima Oakenleaf's impatience slowly rising in the back of her mind.

Chapter Three

Alar Reave entered the courtyard glasshouse to find Farmer Wurst already hard at work. "I could never be a farmer," he said, by way of a greeting. "You lot start way too early in the morning for me."

Farmer Wurst laughed. "Yes. It's not for everyone, my lord. But if you want happy, healthy plants, and a good harvest, what can you do?"

Reave placed his hand lovingly on a nearby tree trunk. "And how goes the harvest, Mr Wurst? As well as can be expected?"

"Better, my lord. Much better. I'd say the trees like their new home very much indeed."

"Good. That's good. We wouldn't want them to be unhappy now would we."

Thunk!

Farmer Wurst frowned. "What was that?"

Thunk!

"There it is again." He looked around. Alar Reave looked up. Farmer Wurst followed his gaze. A shadow passed over their heads. A handful of somethings dropped from the sky.

Thunk, tha-thunk, thunk!

Alar Reave shook his head. "An annoyance, nothing more," he said. "I'll take care of it."

Glunda climbed the ladder from the underground food store beneath her house to her kitchen. She opened all the cupboards to see what was there, then went back down into the food store, stared at the half empty shelves for a little while, then went outside to consider her tiny vegetable patch. She shook her head. There was no two ways about it; no matter how economical she was, no matter how many thin stews and peel soups she made, she didn't have enough to survive the winter. And, worst of all, she didn't have any money in the little tin on the mantle to buy any more.

Glunda went back inside. She needed money, and she needed it fast. Vegetables were selling at an alarming rate down in the market, so she'd been told, and for astronomical prices for this time of year. It seemed the mages, not content with humiliating the Veg Witches by not handing over the Golden Key, were trying to take away the witches' source of power as well. They were buying up vegetables left right and centre, paying three times their worth regardless of how good they were. A sack of mealy spuds was fetching a week's wages, and the price of pumpkins was astronomical. If Glunda didn't get in there soon there'd be no vegetables left, whether she had any money to buy them with or not.

Glunda plonked herself down in her favourite armchair and started to Think.

Everyone 'thinks', but only a witch knows how to Think properly. Most people think with their hearts, making decisions not only on what is true, but on what they *want* to be true. Witches had to learn to only see the unvarnished truth, no matter how harsh it may be. It wasn't fun, and it often led you to conclusions that you'd rather it had not, but seeing things as they Actually Are was the only way you could really help people, and what use was a witch if she couldn't help others in their time of need?

But this wasn't someone else's time of need, was it? It was Glunda's.

Glunda stamped her foot in frustration, not because she couldn't see what needed to be done, but because she could and she didn't like it. It would be humiliating, but she didn't see that she had any other choice.

With an angry sigh, Glunda fished her knitting bag out from under her chair. Digging out a bundle of multicoloured embroidery threads, she got to work.

Market day in Wellety Vale always was a jolly affair. The largest village for miles around (more of a town really, but don't let them hear you saying that), it was where everyone went to sell their wares. And it wasn't just the local farmers either. From hand-sewn clothes to home-made pies, anyone who had anything they wanted rid of would be out before the frost thawed, setting up their covered stalls and trestle tables, ready for when the crowds came.

In the centre of Market Square, in a rectangular gap amongst the neat rows of paying stallholders, were the folk who *really* needed the money. They would set out their blankets of trinkets and toys and sit all day with a ready smile, hoping to make enough to see them through until next week. It was a hard life in the Vale for those without land, but they never complained, even when they saw the pity in their customers' eyes. Why would they? They had never known anything else.

It was towards this square of hope that Glunda strode in a determined way, a large canvas bag over her shoulder.

She smiled and nodded to a few of the locals along the way. "Good morning, Farmer Grey. Your wife has been making her famous pies again, I see."

"Indeed, Mistress Ashwillow."

"Mrs Merton, hello. And how is young Ayal doing?"

"Fine, thank you, Mistress. That ointment you gave her worked a right treat, so it did."

"See. I told you she'd be back on her feet in no time, did I not?"

"That you did, miss, that you did."

Glunda found herself a nice spot right in the middle of the square. There was no point being shy about this. If she was going to humiliate herself in public she may as well do it right out in the open for all to see.

Pulling a tartan blanket from her bag, she set it out neatly on the cold, hard ground. Sitting herself at one end, she began setting out rows of friendship bracelets, dream catchers, and cotton coin purses with button-down flaps, being careful to keep the rows all nice and neat. She ignored the nudges and whispers she heard going on around her. She was a witch, and as far as she was concerned a witch could do whatever she liked, even if that meant competing for coppers with those that could ill afford to lose them.

It wasn't her first time there, trying to make ends meet by selling the things she had made, but it was her first time since putting on the big black hat. She had thought those days were behind her, scrimping and scraping to support the family (it was one of the reasons she had become a witch in the first place) but apparently not. Still, there was nothing to be done now. She was there, so she'd just have to make the best of it, same as everyone else.

A little old lady came over, a look of benign curiosity etched upon her all too innocent face. "Well now. If it isn't little Glunda. Haven't seen you here in a while. Not selling nothing, leastways."

Glunda smiled the smile she kept only for her most troublesome customers. "Good morning, Miss Gleen. And how are we today?"

Eustice Gleen was known throughout the land as the busybody's busybody. The owner of the local bakery, she spent more time sticking her nose into other people's business than she ever did baking her daily bread, and whilst it could be infuriating to find yourself quietly quizzed on the most intimate aspects of your life, it was generally agreed that if Eustice Gleen didn't want to know what you were up to, then what you were up to probably wasn't worth doing in the first place. "Oh, can't complain. Can't complain," said Eustice, picking up one of Glunda's coin purses. "Life could be so much worse, after all. Wouldn't you say, Glunda?"

"That is often the case," said Glunda, expectantly.

Eustice Gleen dropped her voice to a conspiratorial whisper. "I 'eard what happened up at the castle. Shocking business, that. Shocking! 'Ow're you getting on, luv? Everything"—she let her gaze wander over Glunda's hastily prepared wares—"alright and that?"

Glunda knew better than to answer a direct question from Eustice Gleen. "The world turns. The seasons change. Life moves on."

"What's that? One of them witchy sayings we hear so much about?"

"Merely an observation, Miss Gleen. Can I help you find anything today?"

Miss Gleen examined the purse in her hand. "Yes. What does this do?"

"Do? It's a purse. You put money in it."

"And it doubles your money, does it?"

"What? No."

"Ah. So there's always a coin inside whenever you opens her up!" Miss Gleen peered into the little purse. She used her bony fingers to dig around in its shallow depths, but it remained stubbornly coin free.

"What *are* you on about, Miss Gleen? It doesn't do any of those things. It's just a coin purse."

"So it's not magic then?"

"Of course not. Why would it be magic?"

"Coz you're a witch, ain't ya? Why would you be sellin' stuff if they ain't magic?"

"Because—" Glunda caught herself just in time. She took the purse out of Miss Gleen's hand and placed it back on the blanket. "Because things don't always happen the way we expect them to, do they?"

Miss Gleen nodded wisely. "I'm with you. I see what's going on." She patted Glunda on the arm. "Don't you worry, lass. Your secret's safe with me." She walked away quickly, like she'd just picked a pocket and needed to swiftly vacate the area.

"Wait. What secret? What do you mean?"

A little girl ran over, getting in between Glunda and the retreating Miss Gleen who had already found a gaggle of farmers' wives with which to resolutely not share anyone's confidence with.

"Um, hello," said Glunda. "And what are you after, my dear?"

The little girl pointed. "Wot's that?"

"That? That's a friendship bracelet."

"'N' wot do you do wiv one'a them then?"

"Well, you give it to someone, as a symbol of how much you like them."

"An' it makes 'em like you back, does it?'

"Maybe."

"Coz there's this boy at school an' he's always mean to me an' I wants 'im to stop."

"Well, you could try giving one to him, I suppose..."

"An' it'll magic 'im into bein' nice?"

"No. It's not magic, sweetheart. It's just... something nice you can do for people."

"But I wants 'im to stop bein' mean. I wants 'im to like me!"

"You can't make people like you, I'm afraid. They either do or they don't."

"Well that's no good. Wot kind of magic is that?"

"It's not magic. It's just—"

"Oh forget it!" the little girl huffed. "You're worse than me mum." And she stormed off with a furious clump clump clump.

"Another satisfied customer," said a hesitant voice. Glunda turned to find Clum standing awkwardly behind her.

"Yes. I'm on a bit of a roll today." She set about straightening her already neat blanket. "Everyone seems to think everything I sell should be magic somehow, like I've got magic to spare or something."

"I guess it's something to do with you being a witch," said Clum. "They're probably wondering what you're doing here selling this if they *ain't* magic, if'n you see what I mean."

"Yes, well, we have your father to thank for that," said Glunda icily. She felt Clum cringe in shame. "I'm sorry. That was uncalled for."

"S'alright," Clum mumbled.

Glunda patted the ground next to her. "Sit with me a while, won't you? I could do with some friendly company."

Clum placed himself next to Glunda at a respectful distance. They sat in silence for a while, watching the milling crowd.

"I'm sorry about yesterday," Clum said finally. "It weren't right what my dad did. He had no call being all mean to you like that, none at all. If my mother were alive..."

Glunda nodded. "She was a good woman your mum. Knew right from wrong and what was what. She brought herself up a good son, even if her choice in husbands was a bit... questionable."

"She was no good at pickin' horses neither," said Clum, smiling. "Never walked away from a point-to-point with more money than she started off with."

Glunda laughed. "Well, we all have our blind spots. I myself—" A shadow fell across Glunda and Clum. Glunda looked up to find two guards from the mage's castle looming over them.

"Mistress Ashwillow? Come with us please."

Clum swallowed loudly. Glunda didn't move. "Oh yes. Where to exactly?"

"Lord Reave wants a word with you."

"Is that so? And this is his idea of an invitation, is it? Very well. Tell Lord Reave that Mistress Ashwillow is busy at the moment, but if she has time later maybe she will pop by, providing nothing important comes up in the meantime."

"I'm afraid you're going to have to come with us *now*, miss," said the taller of the two guards, taking a step forwards. "Lord Reave was quite insistent about that." He reached out a hand towards Glunda, aiming for her neck, only for it to freeze in mid-air. He looked confused as an icy pins-and-needles sensation crept slowly up his arm. He tried to pull his hand away but it was stuck fast, as if clamped in an invisible vice.

Glunda raised a clawed hand into the air. "Insistent, was he? And did he tell you what happens to people who try to 'insist' themselves upon witches, especially in front of a large crowd?" Glunda tightened her magical grip and the guard fell to his knees. "Somehow I don't think that came up. What do you think, Arfur? Do you think Lord Reave was as insistent as your friend here?"

The shorter of the two guards removed his helmet and smiled weakly. "No, Mistress Ashwillow. In fact, I'm pretty sure he wasn't."

"No. I didn't think so. How's your mother, by the way? Feeling any better, is she?"

"Much better, thank you, Mistress."

"Do give her my regards next time you see her."

"Of course, Mistress. You have my word." The taller guard's lips were starting to turn blue, and there was a faint fogginess to his breath. "Um, Mistress, would you mind letting Trayvah go? Only he ain't lookin' too well."

"Of course, Arfur. You only had to ask." Glunda dropped her hand and Trayvah fell to the ground, clutching his arm. Arfur helped him unsteadily to his feet.

"Thank you, Mistress. An', if'n you have a moment, and you fancies it like, if you could stop by the castle an' 'ave a word with Lord Reave, it would be much appreciated."

Glunda smiled warmly. "Of course. It would be my pleasure." She turned to the other guard. "You see that, Trayvah? That is how you ask someone for a favour." Glunda climbed to her feet. "Clum, I wonder if you wouldn't mind taking care of my things for me? I better see these two home. One of them is looking quite unwell."

"Oh! Um, absolutely, Mistress Ashwillow. I ain't got nuthin'– That is to say, I don't– I mean—"

"A yes will suffice," said Glunda.

"Yes, Mistress Ashwillow."

"Thank you, Clum." Glunda rounded on the two guards. "Right, come on, you two. Let's get you home before you gets yourself into any more trouble."

Glunda followed the Major Domo into the castle's glassed-in courtyard, munching on some left-over roast potatoes as she went. Her little display in Market Square had really taken it out of her, and she had a feeling she'd need her strength for whatever was coming next. And judging by the look on Alar Reave's face, her feeling was right on the money.

"Lord Reave!" she exclaimed before the Major Domo had a chance to introduce her. "What a pleasant surprise. And how are we on this fine morning?"

"Not happy, Glunda. Not happy at all."

The mage dismissed his servant with a quick flick of the head, the Major Domo leaving in a bit of a huff. Announcing people was his favourite part of the job.

"Oh no, Alar. Whatever's the matter?"

The mage pointed up into the sky. Hovering above the glass roof were a handful of rocks, each floating on a disc of rippling red light, surrounded by a smattering of broken bottle pieces. "Pigeons?" said Glunda.

"Witches," said Lord Reave.

Glunda shook her head. "They're too small to be witches."

"I meant they were put there by witches. Or thrown there, should I say."

"Really? And what makes you say that?"

"Because I was there when it happened. I saw them do it."

"Saw who do it, exactly?"

"I... I can't rightly say. You all look the same to me. But it was one of your lot, I'm sure. I could hear the cackling from here."

Glunda chuckled. Such cheap jibes. He really was desperate to get a rise out of her.

She watched as a castle servant, who obviously had drawn the short straw, appeared on the parapet above, clutching a dustpan and brush. Lowering himself over the side, he gingerly placed a foot on whatever the mage's had conjured up to protect the roof, edging his way slowly out into fresh air, rippling plates of red light blossoming beneath his every tentative step.

"You need to have a word with whoever did this, Glunda. Make sure they don't do it again."

"Do I now? And what if I don't? What happens then?"

Alar hesitated. He had to choose his next words very carefully. "The senior mages are furious. They consider this an affront to their authority. There's no telling what they might do if it were to ever happen again."

Glunda deliberately ate another roast potato. Alar Reave reached for an apple in his robe pocket. "That almost sounds like a threat, Alar. Is that what you're doing? Are you threatening me? Because you might want to have a word with your man Trayvah before you go doing something like that, see how trying to push people around has worked out for him so far."

Alar Reave frowned. "Who's Trayvah?"

Glunda shook her head. "Anyway, even if I did know who was responsible, which I don't, there's no guarantee they'd stop just because I said so. It's not like with you wizards, y'know. Witches don't have what you might call a rigid command structure. We're a bit more free-thinking than that." Alar said nothing. He still had his hand in his robe pocket. "However, if you were to see sense and hand over the key, then maybe I could persuade everyone that causing trouble was not in our best interests at this time."

Alar sneered. "I don't think so."

Glunda shrugged. "Then it's out of my hands. You'll have to sort your problems out on your own." She turned and headed for the door. "But I'd be careful about doing anything drastic if I were you. We witches may go our own way day-to-day, but when it comes to trouble we stand as one."

She turned to glare at Alar. "And the Gods help you when we do."

Glunda marched through the woods, her witch boots kicking rocks into the undergrowth. The wood's tiny creatures scurried for safety, knowing better than to get in the way of a witch's wrath.

Damn you, Jemima Oakenleaf, and your damned rocks! What on Earth were you thinking? Did you think you'd smash a few windows and that'd be the end of it? How stupid can you get! She needed to lay off the medicine, that's what she needed to do. It was making her soft between the ears. Glunda would have to have a word with her, of course, she didn't have any choice. They couldn't have witches running about causing havoc all over the place. She hated that it had to be done, and she hated that Alar-bloody-Reave was the one who had asked her to do it. She'd have been fine if it had been anybody else, but Alar Reave!!

Glunda arrived home to find Clum sat on her doorstep, her tartan blanket next to him. As she pushed through her squeaky wooden gate, Clum scrambled to his feet. "I brought your things, Mistress. I only managed to sell about half of them, but I got a good price I reckon."

"You sold some? But I... I didn't expect you to sell them for me. Just keep an eye on them."

"Oh! I'm sorry. I thought it might help. I just..." Clum handed Glunda a fistful of money. "I think I did alright for you."

Glunda counted out the many coins. It was almost as much as she had expected to get for the entire lot, let alone half. "You did wonderfully, Clum. I'm impressed. You must tell me how you did it. Come, a haul such as this will get you a cup of tea if nothing else."

In Glunda's living room, Clum sat on the edge of his seat, his hands in his lap. Glunda brought him his tea, half a dozen biscuits jammed onto the saucer along with it. "Thank you, Mistress Ashwillow. Very kind."

"Clum, we've known each other since school. We used to play Brentish Bulldogs in the school yard every lunchtime. I think we can dispense with the Mistress, don't you?"

"Right. It's just, ever since you became a witch, it's hard to know what's right and what's wrong, eh."

Glunda made herself comfy in the chair opposite. "I'll tell you what, when I'm not wearing the hat, and there's no one else around, how about you call me Glunda, like you used to?"

"Okay, Glunda."

"Great. And relax, will you. You're acting like you're having tea at your rich aunt's house or something."

Clum smiled as he turned slightly red. Sitting back in his chair, he set about to some serious dunking.

Glunda let him get two biscuits in before saying what was on her mind. She didn't have to wait long. "Clum, can I ask you something?" Clum, his mouth full of soggy biscuit, nodded. "Why did so many farms turn on us? And so quickly too. Have we not been good to people? Provided for them when they were in need? Helped them grow and prosper, season in and season out? And to side with the mages, of all people. What are they thinking? You cannot trust a mage. They will betray you soon as look at you!"

She half expected Clum to bolt for the door when faced with such direct questioning, but instead he looked thoughtful and sad.

"I guess it's just, like, people don't like being told what to do, even if it's good for them. Like when you were a kid and your mum told you not to eat too many sweets or you'd get stomach ache. You did what you were told because you had to, but given half a chance you'd have eaten all the sweets you could and not thought twice about it." Glunda nodded. How many times had she done things she wasn't meant to just for the hell of it? "And as for the mages, they're offering good money and making all kinds of promises to get folks on side. They reckon they can do everything the witches did, and at half the price. For a lot of folks that was too good an offer to turn down."

"But they know nothing about fecunding the land or the granting of Favours. They'll mess it all up, and that'll be an entire harvest wasted. What'll folks do then, when the food starts running out?"

"Knowing my dad and his mates, if that happens there'll be a few mages finding out what the pointy end of a pitchfork feels like."

"Ha! And it'll serve them right an' all." Glunda munched on a biscuit, a cruel gleam in her eye. "I just hope they don't come round here expecting us to save them. You makes your bed, you lie in it, far as I'm concerned."

Clum looked at her with great sadness. "Yeah. I guess so, eh."

CHAPTER FOUR

Winter. The wind howled through the castle, squeezing through every crack and crevice with a high-pitched whine. Ignoring the chill in the air, and the barrage of snow rushing sideways past his window, Alar Reave took a bite of apple and concentrated on the box of dirt before him. He visualised the seed, the soil surrounding it, the water in between. He saw it grow in his mind, turning into a tall vine, heavy with runner beans. Checking his notes, he said the words he'd been working on for the past four hours, altering the inflection just slightly to see if maybe this time he could get the spell to work properly.

The box of dirt exploded, covering Alar Reave in soggy manure. Wiping the mulch from his eyes, he went to retrieve his broom, sweeping the shards of his latest experiment into the corner of the room with all the rest.

He opened the door to his chambers. "Cheeves! Another box, if you please. And make this one slightly less dank, if you wouldn't mind. My rug will never be clean again at this rate."

There was a knock at Glunda's door. She pulled it open, a flurry of snow and wind invading the cosy warmth within. A figure entered, hunched against the harsh weather. Glunda pushed the door closed behind them.

"By 'eck!" said the visitor, stamping the snow off her boots. "It's colder than a witch's"—the visitor caught Glunda's eye—"tip... a witch's tip, out there. Like, the tip of her hat, when it gets cold, if you know what I mean?"

"I do indeed, Mrs Bulshanks. I do indeed," said Glunda tactfully. "May I take your coat?"

The visitor shed her outer layer to reveal a robust woman used to going about her daily business with a calf under each arm. The cold had made her face red, but then again everything made her face red. Mrs Bulshanks's complexion was always either flushed, ruddy, refreshed, or rosy-cheeked, depending on what time of year it was, and quite often what time of day it was as well.

"Won't you have a seat?"

"Very kind of you, lass. I've, er, brought you some veggies to be getting on with." Mrs Bulshanks pointed to the two bags she had deposited by the front door. "I figured you might be needing them, what with the weather being how it is an' that."

"That's very generous of you, Mrs Bulshanks. And most welcome. One could always use a few more vegetables for the pot, eh."

"Tha's got that right," said Mrs Bulshanks.

Truth be told, Glunda had no idea what she was going to do with Mrs Bulshanks's donation. She'd had more than a few late night visits these past weeks, all with some vegetables for her, and all with a request of some kind. Her cupboards and cold store were full to bursting, and even the drawer under her bed was getting more and more difficult to slide shut these days.

"And how are you in yourself, Mrs Bulshanks? Are you well?"

"Can't complain, Glunda. Can't complain. It's my Danis who ain't himself."

Glunda was not surprised. "Really? How so?"

"Well now, what's the best way to put it? He's not what you might call very amorous at the moment. In the bedroom area, if you know what I mean?"

"Oh! I see."

"Only it's not like him, not wanting his... amour. Normally we amour every other night, but lately it's been, like, once or twice a month at best."

"That does sound... difficult. Um, have you spoken to him about it? Perhaps he's not as interested in such things as he once was. Or maybe he thinks that seven children is enough, and there's no need to go making any more." Glunda remembered seeing Mr Bulshanks down the market the other week, with just half of his expanding brood in tow. The poor man looked exhausted. "I imagine one's ardour lessens somewhat over time."

"Listen, lass, no offence, but you ain't married. You don't know what it's like. A married woman needs her ardour or she's like to go potty, and I ain't had a good ardouring in a long time. Is there not something you can do? Something that'll... get his ardour up a bit?"

Glunda went over to the sideboard. She pulled it open to reveal an array of premixed potions, each with an instruction label tied around its neck. Witches didn't sell their magic. That would be unethical, not to mention highly embarrassing. They did however sometimes provide potions and tinctures for their friends and family when they came to visit, especially when said friends brought them the gift of a few bags of vegetables. It would be rude not to.

It had started with something to help the stomach of the little girl down the lane. Her father had been extremely generous in his appreciation of Glunda's help. Then it was Miss Gleen who had needed help with a gangrenous toe. That had really gotten the word out. Pretty soon there was a queue of people at Glunda's door, all with arms full of vegetables and all looking for her assistance in one way or another. It wasn't payment, you understand, they weren't paying her, but if her appreciation for their generosity was expressed in a way that only a witch could, well, who could have a problem with that, eh?

The fact was Glunda was doing better now than she ever had as a 'normal' witch, and she wasn't the only one. Rumour had it that most of the witches were happy to exchange Favours for a small donation, provided the donation came first of course. Even Mistress Hearthcrow had been seen handing out bottles to visitors when she thought no one was looking... allegedly.

It wasn't selling magic. A witch would never sell her magic. It was just... making the best of a bad situation.

Glunda didn't have what Mrs Bulshanks was after, she knew she didn't. Such a potion did not exist (although it was amazing how many people were convinced it did). But she couldn't send the woman away empty handed. She had her reputation to think of. Adding some almond oil to a generous amount of clarified butter, she mixed up a batch of something that, whilst not magic, ought to work just as well.

"Here we are. Extract of Gensing root mixed with Hohoba oil."

Mrs Bulshanks scowled at the (to her eyes) tiny bottle. "And this'll work, will it?"

"Absolutely it will."

"Aye, well, I'll take your word for love. I'm willing to try anything at this point."

"Don't worry. Simply massage it into the... offending area and his, er, ardour, will be up and about in no time."

The castle's Great Hall was awash with a sea of greedy, slurping, munching sounds, punctuated by the odd belch or growl of digestive distress. The senior Drupe Mages were at lunch, a festival of gluttony that might take a few hours or which could go on for the rest of the day depending on if there was pudding or not.

Alar Reave entered, trying not to show his disgust at the unabashed greed he saw before him. There was as much food on the floor as there was on the table, never mind what had made it down the front of most of the mages' shabby robes. None of the men round the table had ever known what it was to go without, and if you had tried to explain the concept of not having enough they would have scoffed at you like you were mad. The average Drupe Mage came from the oldest of old money. As far as they were concerned, if you didn't have food on your table it was only because you didn't have the guts to take someone else's.

At the head of the table, Lord Feffle spotted Alar picking his way between all the gnawed-on bones, discarded salad, and stray dollops of mashed potato. "Ah! Lord Reave. How goes the experimentation?" Lord Feffle regarded all the dirt down the front of Alar's tunic. "Winning, are we?"

Alar Reave toed a piece of pork pie crust out of the way. "No, my lord. Not at all. My results have been a little explosive so far to be of any use."

Lord Feffle laughed, spraying chicken grease over the mage closest to him. "Chin up, lad! We're not licked yet. I'm sure you'll get the hang of it before the thaws come."

"Yes, well, with that in mind, sir, perhaps yourself or one of our esteemed colleagues here might deign to give me a hand? The spring thaws are awful close after all."

Lord Feffle dismissed the suggestion with a wave of his greasy hand. "The spring thaw is miles away. We've plenty of time. I have every confidence in you, Lord Reave. I'm sure you'll figure it out eventually." He tossed Alar a drumstick. "Come, lad, get yourself something to eat. You need to keep your strength up. All this worry is bad for the constitution, you know."

Alar placed the drumstick back on the table. "Thank you, my lord, but I cannot stay. There is much still to be done."

Lord Feffle gave a disinterested shrug. "Suit yourself," he said, jamming the entire discarded drumstick into his mouth and sucking the bone clean. "Any more of that Truscan red? Lord Kane, the bottle is with you, sir! Pass it round, pass it round. Don't be stingy, what."

Taking this to mean he was dismissed, Alar Reave quietly left the room.

CHAPTER FIVE

Alar Reave stood in the empty field wishing more than anything that he was somewhere else. The sky was bright, the air clear, and all along the hedgerows snowdrops had begun to poke their heads out to see what was going on. Spring was on its way, and whilst it hadn't sprung yet, it was certainly getting ready to do away with winter any day now.

"Thank you for letting me use your field, Farmer Miggins. It is much appreciated."

"Not at all, my lord. Glad to help," said Clum's father.

"Bit early to be preppin' the land, innit?" said Clum, rather too loudly. "It's not even the equinox yet."

"Quiet, boy! His lordship knows what he's doing."

Let's hope, thought Alar, munching on a banana as he prepared to cast what the other mages in the castle had taken to calling his Charm of Fecundment.

Alar rolled up his sleeves. Raising his hands in the air, he began to chant, forming the idea of growth in his mind as his fingers formed the precise mudras needed to make the spell work. He felt the power well within him, flowing out through his hands to blanket the entire field. With a final flourish, he broke the connection, letting the energy settle on the land to be absorbed, ready for when the rains came.

Alar smiled, pleased with the result. It had gone better than he thought it would. Definitely better than it had in practise. Nothing had blown up for a start.

"Is that it, my lord?" said Clum's father. "Only that ain't exactly 'ow the witches does it, if'n you don't mind my sayin'. Not that I'm complaining or owt, only I needs to be sure. My livelihood sort of depends on it, y'see."

"Don't you worry, Farmer Miggins. All is well. You just plant your seed as normal, and I guarantee you—" Alar suddenly got a funny feeling in the pit of his stomach. He turned to the field, looking worried. "Um, you might want to back up a little," he said, retreating swiftly towards the nearest hedgerow.

"Why? What's gonna—"

With a gut-shaking *whumf!* the field erupted in flame, the bare earth becoming an instant sea of green fire. It sent the three men running for cover, scrambling over the hedgerow (and each other) to save their hides (and eyebrows) from the intense heat.

One by one they poked their heads over the top of the hedge to watch the field burning merrily away, its brown earth slowly turning a dark, crispy shade of black, like burnt toast only much, much worse.

"Is it supposed to do that?" said Clum.

Alar Reave pulled a multitude of faces as he ran through a list of equally implausible excuses in his head. "Well, you see..." he began, but then he immediately gave up. Some situations you can't put a positive spin on, no matter how hard you try. "No," he said, his shoulders slumped in defeat. "No it is not."

On a hill overlooking Farmer Miggins's field, Glunda and Ellsa sat on Glunda's tartan blanket having a picnic. They munched on cucumber sandwiches and drank elderflower cordial as they watched the distant field burn.

Ellsa sat wide eyed, a sandwich halfway to her hanging-open mouth. "Goodness!"

"Yup."

"Is it meant to do that, do you think?"

"Judging by the way Farmer Miggins is jumping up and down, I doubt it." Glunda would have to thank Clum later for warning her about this morning's activities. This was useful information to have. "Come on, Ellsa, eat up. We've a conclave to get to."

Ellsa dutifully scoffed down her sandwich, reaching for another as she took a healthy swig of cordial.

Coven Wood stood at the centre of everything. Equal distance from any border or shoreline, it was where the witches of the land came to air their grievances and talk things out (when they weren't descending on some poor witch's house to eat all her food and berate her with their unqualified opinion, that is). Glunda and Ellsa arrived to find the path into the wood already well-trodden by a multitude of boot prints.

"We're late!" said Ellsa, sounding worried.

Glunda chuckled. "Don't worry, Ellsa. I'm the Keeper of the Cauldron, remember? They wouldn't dare start without me."

They arrived at the clearing in the centre of the woods to find ten witches sitting around a healthy bonfire, all in various states of agitation, with Mistress Marleena Hearthcrow holding court. She seemed to be doing her best to let everyone have their say without letting any of the more vocal witches, like Jemima Oakenleaf, drown out any of the more sober ones — of which there didn't seem to be many, since some genius had decided to bring a barrel of cider with them.

Mistress Hearthcrow was stood in front of the Cauldron Keeper's seat, with the Great Ladle in hand. She didn't seem to notice Glunda's arrival. Or if she did, she didn't seem to care. "Ladies, please. We won't get anywhere fighting amongst ourselves. We must be united if we are to— Oh, hello, Glunda."

"What's going on? Did you... Did you start without me?"

"Not at all. We were just... chatting until you arrived. No harm in that, is there?"

Glunda noticed a few of the older witches nudging each other and winking. She walked up to Mistress Hearthcrow and held out her hand. "Thank you, Mistress Hearthcrow. I'll take it from here."

Marleena Hearthcrow hesitated, then she handed over the ladle. "But of course, dear. Here you go."

Mistress Hearthcrow went to sit on the empty stool to the right of Glunda's seat. "Not there," said Glunda without turning. "That's Ellsa's spot."

Marleena Hearthcrow paused. She felt the eyes of everyone upon her. Finally, she nodded as graciously as she could. "As the Keeper commands," she said, somewhat reluctantly.

Glunda nodded Ellsa angrily to her seat, as Mistress Hearthcrow went to sit with the rest of the elder witches (who had all chosen to sit near the cider barrel for some unknown reason).

The conclave was made up mostly of elder witches, with just a handful Glunda and Ellsa's age. They sat on the opposite side of the fire to the cider barrel, not saying much of anything, but unlike nervous children at the grownups table, it was a witchy kind of quiet, the kind where you watched and waited to see what was going to happen before chiming in. All witches, no matter their age, were more than happy to speak their mind, but a wise witch, a witch with a head on her shoulders, was careful about when she spoke her mind, how much, and to whom.

There was a small black cauldron hanging next to the fire, beside where Glunda was standing. Traditionally it contained vegetable soup, for the witches to share when the conclave was over. From the smell of it, someone was using it to make mulled wine. Glunda banged on the side of the cauldron to call the meeting to order.

"Ladies, thank you all for coming. We have much to discuss. Now, as I'm sure you're all aware, the equinox is almost upon us, meaning that soon spring will be here."

"Tell us something we don't know," said one of the elder witches.

"It is only a matter of time before the people turn to us for the traditional fecunding of the land. We must decide, as a group, what our response will be."

"Sod 'em," said Jemima Oakenleaf. "Ain't none of oor business anyhow. The mages're in charge. Let them sort it oot."

"What about the mages?" said Alayah Buckthorn, the youngest witch there. "Rumour has it they're working on a way to fecund the land themselves. Maybe the people won't need us."

"Oh, I don't think we have much to worry about in that regard," said Glunda. "Ellsa and I just witnessed their attempts in action. I think it's safe to say they won't be making a significant contribution to the coming harvest in this, or any other year."

"What makes you say that?"

"Because they set the field on fire!" said Ellsa suddenly.

"What?"

"Yes! It was all green flame and everything. And when it was finished, the soil was all black!"

The elder witches burst into laughter. The younger witches exchanged worried looks. Glunda frowned an excited Ellsa into silence. She banged on the cauldron once more. "What Mistress Puddleglump tells you is true. Not only have some of the mages' attempts at fecunding gone badly, but they have actually made the ground worse. We may be looking at a difficult growing season for many unless we intervene."

Jemima Oakenleaf lunged to her feet. "And why should we, when thems that used to be oor frien's went an' turnt their backs on us? We never did nothin' to them, yet they went an' sided with the Drupe Mages first chance they got! Why should we help them that's got no interest in helpin' us, I ask you?"

"Because it's what we do," said Alayah Buckthorn calmly. "We are witches, and a witch helps those that needs it, whether they want us to or not."

"Pah!" grumbled Jemima Oakenleaf, as she was persuaded gently back into her seat.

Marleena Hearthcrow rose to standing. "May I speak, Glunda?" Glunda gestured with the ladle for her to go on. Marleena turned to Alayah Buckthorn. "You are quite right, Mistress Buckthorn, it is our job as witches to help people. But sometimes it is necessary for people to realise just how much they need your help before any such help can be given.

After all, you can warn a child a thousand times not to burn themselves on an open fire, but it is only once they do burn themselves that they finally listen to you."

"What are you saying, Mistress Hearthcrow?" said Glunda.

"Only that perhaps we should allow this difficult harvest to come to pass. Let the people reap the benefits of their own decisions, then maybe, when the autumnal equinox comes around, they will find themselves keen to have the Golden Key in the correct hands once more."

"Let the crops fail, you mean? Let the people go hungry?"

"Only a little. They won't starve. A normal harvest is still a pretty good harvest to those who manage without our help."

A murmur of approval rippled through the elder witches. The last six months had been hard for them, despite the impressive amount of vegetables they had been able to amass by not selling their magic to the highest bidder. Maybe it was time for the people to feel some of that hardship as well.

Marleena Hearthcrow took her seat, as all eyes turned to Alayah Buckthorn. Realising she had somehow become the spokesperson for the younger witches, Alayah stood reluctantly. "I hear what the illustrious mistress has to say, and I do not disagree with any of it, but when has what someone else does been a measure for what we choose to do? A witch is not a weathervane blowing in the wind, but the very wind itself."

"Ooh! Hark at her, giving out lessons in witchery all of a sudden!" The elder witches laughed.

"Nevertheless," Aliyah continued, "it is up to us to decide what needs to be done. And if it's a choice between helping people or watching them starve I know which I'd prefer." She sat down again to the sound of more than one raspberry blown in her direction.

"Quite right," said Glunda. "Well said. So, with that in mind, here's what I think we should do..."

"Ach, here we go," said Jemima Oakenleaf, whose love of the cider was starting to get the better of her. "Glunda's gonna tell us how the world works. Get ready, girls. Tha's aboot to learn summat 'ere."

A few of the elder witches chuckled. Glunda gripped the iron ladle tightly. She looked to Mistress Hearthcrow, but she seemed more interested in examining her nails than in coming to Glunda's defence. She wasn't in a huff, because witches didn't huff, but after being publicly put in her place she clearly wasn't in the mood to do Glunda any favours either. The question was, did she intend to do her harm instead? If there's one thing the elder witches knew well it was how to hold a grudge. Rumour was some of them had even taken lessons in it, back in the day.

"I'll thank you to show a bit more respect for the Keeper of the Cauldron, Mistress Oakenleaf. It was you all that put me here in the first place."

Jemima Oakenleaf scoffed. "Aye, and what a mistake *that* turned oot tae be. Lost us the Golden Key right out'a the gate, din'cha? Hard tae respect a lassie wot done that, wouldn't tha say?"

The clearing fell silent. Even the birds held their breath. It had been a long time since two witches had done battle, decades really, and whilst no one wanted to see anyone get hurt (not in any serious way anyway) they all kind of wanted to see what a proper witch battle actually looked like.

"Why not have a vote?" said Mistress Hearthcrow innocently. Everyone turned to gape. A vote? Witches didn't vote. Votes were for people who couldn't make up their own minds, and no witch had ever had any problem making up their own mind, ever.

"Aye! Good idea," said Mistress Oakenleaf.

"Yes. Let's have a vote," another elder witch added, followed by a chorus of voices from the cider side of the fire.

"A vote!"

"Yes, a vote."

"Let's have a vote!"

Glunda turned to the young witches in astonishment, but they were all as bemused as she was. Then she caught sight of the look in Mistress Hearthcrow's eye.

"Very well," she managed, through gritted teeth. "We shall have a vote."

Of course it was only once the vote was cast that the real

shouting began. The elder witches accused the younger witches of knowing nothing about being a witch, whilst the younger witches said the elder witches had forgotten how. Rude gestures were made and mugs were thrown, and it took someone (it was Glunda) accidentally kicking the mulled wine into the fire, flinging spiced sludge and ash everywhere, for the whole debacle to finally break up. The witches left by broom and boot, leaving just Glunda and Marleena Hearthcrow alone in the clearing.

Glunda looked around at the mess she had made. "Well, you got what you wanted."

"Me?" said Mistress Hearthcrow, her hand to her chest. "I didn't do anything. Merely tried to help you out of a bad spot."

"A vote. Like that was ever going to solve anything."

"But it did though, didn't it? We needed a way forward, and now we have one." Mistress Hearthcrow flicked some mud off the hem of her dress. "Speaking of which, I do hope you will abide by the conclave's decision. It would be awfully embarrassing, not to mention insulting, for the Keeper of the Cauldron to go against the will of the witches."

Glunda seethed. "Don't worry about me, *Mistress* Hearthcrow. I will do what is expected of me, of that you can have no doubt!"

CHAPTER SIX

S pring. The equinox came and went, not that anybody noticed. Even the Drupe Mages, who normally had a big party to celebrate, were too busy counting their money and planning on ways to make even more to care. Only Glunda took note of the changing of the season. With the end of winter came the end of her supposed tenure as Keeper of the Cauldron. She would remain in the position until the next keeper was named, of course, but whereas the position had meant very little before due to the Drupe Mages' shenanigans, it meant even less now.

In the middle of nowhere, next to a crossroads that used to be well travelled but was now just the place where two roads had a dispute about which was the best way to go, stood The Ploughed Furrow. The Furrow was a tavern of no repute. It contained good beer, bad food, and a clientele for whom a layer of dirt was considered the minimum dress code. It was where all the local farmers came to wash the dust out of their throats after a hard day's work, and but for their patronage it would have crumbled to dust itself long ago. But endure it did, and in doing so had become such a staple of the local's lives that the peasants who lived within shouting distance didn't go out of a weekend to get ploughed, they went out of a weekend to get furrowed.

As the sun went down, Clum followed his father into the tavern. It had been a long day of sowing seed, and the pair of them were so dead on their feet they barely paused to knock the dirt off their boots.

Walking wearily to the bar, Clum's father threw a few nods to the regulars they passed along the way. Ordering himself a pint and Clum a shandy — Clum would have preferred a pint too, but he didn't have any say in the matter — he turned to the two men propping up the bar beside him. "Shan, Shaymus. Good to see ya."

"And yourself, Clem. How's the seeding out going?"

"About done, Shaymus. About done. Reckon we'll be finished by the end of the week. And yourself?"

"Aye, same. Got one more field to get to then that's us finished."

Clum's father took a long swig of his pint. "And what about the Drupe Mages? Has't tha had any joy out of them?"

"Some, some. I wouldn't be surprised if'n we have a good harvest this year coz of 'em. Knock on wood, o' course." Shaymus rapped his fist on the countertop.

"So they never set your field on fire or owt? Well, that's lucky. And what about you, Shan? Any trouble your end with 'em?"

Shan shared a look with his friend. "Oh, er, no. No, not at all. They, um, seemed to do alright, like."

Clum took a half step back as his father snorted angrily. He'd been in a foul mood ever since Alar's visit, which was several weeks ago now. It made him prone to lashing out, usually in Clum's direction.

"Well, you're both braver than me," growled Farmer Miggins. "After what they did to my top field I'd not have 'em back for love nor money."

Shaymus and Shan shared another significant look. "Have you not thought about asking your witch to help out at all? You might find her quite amenable... for the right price."

Farmer Miggins sneered. "It'll be a long time afore I go crawlin' on me hands and knees to that lot again, let me tell you."

"Maybe I could ask?" said Clum bravely. "I'm sure Glunda... I mean Mistress Ashwillow, would be more than happy to do us a favour this one time."

Clem Miggins glared at his son. "You'll do no such thing! And I'll thank you to keep your opinions to yourself, lad. This here's men's talk. You get away into the corner with your mates. This conversation ain't for the likes of you."

Biting his lip, Clum took his drink over to a table in the corner where Jayce and Eli, Shaymus and Shan's two boys, sat sullenly sipping their own adulterated ales.

"Got banished an' all, did you?" said Jayce.

"Yeah, but it's fine. My dad's about to go off on one about witches and I can't be done with that."

"He doesn't like them, does he? Makes you think he must have gone out with a witch when he were a young lad or something."

Eli chuckled.

"So I hear you've had some joy with the mages over at your place?" said Clum. "Got your land all fertile and that."

Both Eli and Jayce laughed. "Is that what they're saying, is it? Well, if that's their story then it must be true." Jayce winked at Eli.

"It's not?"

"Oh, we had the mages round alright. Blew up our best pumpkin patch they did."

"Same here," said Eli.

"So what's he telling my dad it all went fine for?"

Jayce gave Clum a knowing grin. "Because when everything starts coming up roses he's going to need a reason as to why."

"They both are," said Eli.

"You mean you've had the witches in? The pair of you."

Jayce and Eli exchanged a knowing look. "Put it this way," said Jayce, "there's at least one witch walking around with more coin in her pocket than you might reasonably expect her to have, if'n you catch my drift?"

Clum did. It was hard not to.

Clum got his father to drop him off on the way home. He said it was because he fancied a walk to clear his head, which was true. What he didn't mention was the route he intended to take on the way back.

Clum arrived at Glunda's cottage to find her hard at work in the garden. She had ripped out most of the flowerbeds, and was now busy turning the lawn into nice, neat furrows of freshly tilled soil. Her skirt was hiked up to keep it out of the dirt, her top, damp with sweat, hung against her in a most distracting way, and her hair, all loose and wild, flew gently in the softly blowing wind. She looked... normal, in a do-you-fancy-going-to-the-village-dance-with-me kind of way, which Clum was not prepared for at all. He had to remind himself not to stare. Terrible things happened to farm boys who stared at witches for too long... or so he had been told.

"Hello, Clum. How lovely to see you."

"Um, yes, hello, Mistress Ashwillow. Lovely to see you too."

"Now, Clum..." said Glunda reproachfully. Clum blushed.

"Sorry, Glunda. It's a hard habit to break."

"That's alright. I understand. What can I do for you?"

"I wanted to ask you something. It's about the, um—" Clum watched Glunda trying to lever a large rock out of the ground. "Do you want a hand with that?"

"You know what, that would be lovely. I started off well, but my get-up-and-go seems to have got-up-and-gone."

"I'm not surprised," said Clum, taking hold of Glunda's shovel. "It looks like you've done a full day's work already."

"Yes, well, had to be done. It's a shame to lose the lawn, but after last winter I wanted to be sure I had enough veggies of my own to see me through. You never know what's going to happen these days, do you?"

"I guess not," grunted Clum, as he dislodged the rock from its earthy home. "Actually, that's, er, kind of what I wanted to talk to you about. Y'see, I was wondering if you fancied popping by the farm and giving it a bit of a—" He waved his hands about in a vaguely magical way. "Only I heard how some of the witches were doing that for some people. For money, like. And though we ain't got much it'd mean a lot to my dad and me if—"

"Hello, Glunda. Clum. Nice to see you both."

Glunda and Clum turned to find Alar Reave stood the other side of Glunda's front gate.

Clum nodded curtly. "Lord Reave."

"Hello, Alar," said Glunda, smoothing down her dress as she tucked a few stray hairs behind her ears. "What can we do you for?" As she spoke, Glunda hastily tugged on the black cardigan she'd left hanging on a nearby bush.

"There was something I wanted to talk to you about." Alar glanced at Clum. "In private, if that's alright."

Clum turned to walk away but Glunda stopped him with a hand on the elbow. "Clum would never betray a confidence. Speak your piece, Lord Reave."

"As you wish," said Alar. "I've come to ask if the witches might be interested in helping out with the spring fecund. Our own efforts have been... modest, to say the least, and we are concerned that this year's harvest may be at risk. We were hoping that you would be up for giving us a hand. For a modest fee, or course."

Glunda looked at Clum. The hope in his face was ten times that of Alar's. She gently shook her head. "I'm sorry, Lord Reave, but we cannot help you. The witches have agreed that we are not going to get involved. The spring fecund is your responsibility, not ours." Beside her, Glunda felt Clum's shoulders slump.

"You won't even do it for the people you claim to serve? What if there's not enough to go around? What will you do then?"

"Oh, don't be so dramatic, Alar. The people will be fine. The harvest might not be as bountiful as it was before, but there will be a harvest. Anyway, it's not them you're concerned about, is it? You're only worried that something will go wrong and it'll be up to you to sort it out. What'll you do then, Lord Reave? Not so much fun being in charge when there's work to be done, is it?"

Lord Reave fumed. "Is that your final word on the matter?"

"It is, yes."

"Very well then."

Turning on his heel, Lord Reave stalked off into the woods.

Glunda looked to Clum, who was busy wrestling the large rock over to the side of the garden. "I'm sorry, Clum. I know that's not what you wanted to hear. I wish I could explain, but it's... it's complicated."

"Doesn't matter," Clum mumbled, not looking at Glunda. "Let's just crack on with getting this veg planted, eh."

Chapter Seven

G lunda was troubled by what Clum had said, so one day she decided to go for a little walk. Packing up a week's worth of food, she put on her toughest hobnail boots, dug out her sturdiest walking stick (the one with the V at the top for you to rest your thumb, which her father had given her for her sixteenth birthday) and set off out the door to see what she could see.

Every witch had a fief and every fief was unique. There were wheat fiefs, and coastal fiefs, and fiefs made up entirely of hills. Valley fiefs, and forest fiefs, and fiefs that snaked through the land like a lost river seeking the sea. Glunda visited them all, and everywhere she went she found something she didn't like. There were sprouting fields of corn too tall for that time of year, pumpkins and potatoes more lush than they had any right to be, and plants growing where those types of plants really shouldn't, the ground being too dry, too clay, or too hard for them to take root. It all had the faint hint of magic about it, and witch magic at that.

Just about the only place she didn't find any obvious signs of interference was Mistress Hearthcrow's domain, although it did seem like every fief bordering hers had been tampered with in some way or another.

As she travelled, Glunda slept rough, making camp wherever she happened to be when the sun went down. She'd bedded down in woods, by streams, on the edge of fields, even in a small cave she'd come across one night, but by the fifth day the novelty was starting to wear thin, so it was with great pleasure that she rounded a bend in the river she'd been following and came across Alayah Buckthorn's winter camp.

If there was one witch whose fief Glunda had great appreciation for (because a wise witch was never envious of others, but instead made the best of what she had) it was Alayah Buckthorn's. With its rolling hills, undulating plains, and herds of wild horses running loose everywhere, you could walk its byways from dawn 'til dusk and never bore of its untamed beauty. Not that Glunda regretted her own fief, you understand. It was where she grew up, where all her friends and family were. Never could a place be more accurately called home. But when you know somewhere like the back of your hand, where every road has a memory and every tree a tale to tell, to be somewhere unknown to you, and you unknown to it, was an allure felt by all at one time or another, even a witch.

Alayah Buckthorn had not grown up in the fief where she now lived. She had grown up somewhere far away, where their customs were strange and their language even stranger. Her last name wasn't even Buckthorn. She'd changed it when it became apparent that her real last name had far too many vowels in it for your average local to wrap their parochial tongue around. Alayah had been persuaded to go there because she was good with horses and she didn't mind the harsh weather that swept the plains when the winds were high. It helped that she was used to such things, and that she had come prepared. Alayah lived in a round white tent with slatted wooden walls and a big red wooden door. Covered in layers of canvas and felt, it was warm in the winter and cool in the summer, with all the home comforts you could ask for, including a bed, a table and chairs, a small library, and a metal stove on which to cook your evening meal. She called it a yurt, and Glunda was very keen to find out what a night beneath its domed roof was going to be like.

Glunda approached the camp to find Mistress Buckthorn sat dangling her bare feet in the fast-flowing river. The water must have been freezing but she didn't seem to mind one bit. "Hullo there in the camp. May I come in?"

"Mistress Ashwillow! What a pleasant surprise. I wasn't expecting you."

"Nor I you, if I am honest, but I'm glad you're here. I did not fancy a night out on the open plains."

Alayah laughed. "Yes, they're not to everyone's tastes. But of course you're welcome to spend the night. Come, sit down. Make yourself comfortable. There's yak's milk tea if you'd like. And some stew on its way, in a little while."

"Thank you. That is most kind." Glunda sniffed the tea but decided against it. It smelt a bit... foreign, even for her experienced palate. Sitting on the ground next to Mistress Buckthorn, she removed her boots and rubbed her tired feet.

"You should stick your feet in the river. It's surprisingly refreshing after a day's walk."

"And cold too, I'll bet," said Glunda.

Alayah laughed again. "Only a little, and not for long. Trust me. I would never lead a fellow witch astray." She winked at Glunda. "Not on purpose anyway."

Ever the gracious guest, Glunda removed her socks. Plunging her feet into the icy water, she gasped. "Crikey! That's... invigorating."

"The best part is when you dry them off. They get all warm without you having to hold them by the fire. It's an old horseman's trick."

"I'll take your word for it."

"So, what brings you to my neck of the woods, Mistress Ashwillow? I don't think I've ever seen you out this way before."

Glunda feigned indifference. "Oh, you know, I just thought I'd have a bit of a wander, see what I could see. You know how it is."

Alayah gave a wry smile. When it came to indifference, Glunda feigned it quite badly. "Yes, that seems to be the done thing for witches around here. I found Mistress Hearthcrow sneaking about the other day as well."

That caught Glunda's attention. From the few conversations she'd had on her travels, Alayah wasn't the only one. "Oh really? And what was she up to? Did she say?"

"Like you, she was out for a wander, seeing what she could see. I did not enquire too deeply. Old folk like going around sticking their noses into other people's business, but they don't like it when you stick your nose back in theirs." Only being a few years older than Alayah, Glunda assumed the 'old folks' comment was directed at Marleena Hearthcrow. "I assumed she was here to make sure I wasn't doing anything she thought I shouldn't," Alayah continued. "As are you, perhaps?"

Glunda saw no point in denying it. "Yes, I suppose I am. I'm sorry. I know how insulting that is. But this is the first time the witches have decided not to bless the land. I guess I was curious to see if people were sticking to that or not."

"And?"

"And they're not, far as I can tell. There's been blessings all over the place! They all deny it, of course, say it must have been someone else, but the signs are clear. It just... it makes no sense. Why have a vote if you're not going to abide by its decision? What's the point?"

"What indeed," said Alayah, extracting her feet from the cold river so she could towel them dry. "You know, back where I am from, we have a saying. A happy horse belongs to everyone, but an unhappy horse is yours and yours alone." Glunda must have looked very confused. "It's meaning is hard to translate. It is something like, when a young horseman who has nothing asks his friends 'How is the herd?' he is talking about the whole herd. All the horses, owned by everyone, and the ones running wild as well. To him, a happy herd is a happy life, no matter where that happiness lies.

"It is only when he gets older, and has horses of his own, that his herd becomes small. Then all he cares about is his little herd. His life becomes tough because he must fight, alone, to keep what is his. Instead of everyone taking care of everything for everyone else, he becomes one man, taking care of a few things, just for himself. It is a sad day when someone who was once free learns the words 'me' and 'mine'. It is the beginning of their burden, and it is a burden that will one day drag them to their grave." Glunda didn't know what to say to that. Alayah Buckthorn looked at her sadly. "No matter. You are troubled, so let me put your mind at rest. I have not interfered with the lands in my fief, as agreed, although, to be honest, I would if called upon to do so. Helping others is our duty after all."

"Are you sure? Only I've seen fields on your land that definitely seemed like they've been tampered with."

Alayah tossed Glunda the towel. "If they were it wasn't by me. Now dry your feet. Tea's almost ready, and I'll not have your traipsing muddy footprints all over my nice clean floor."

The woods at night were cold and dark, but seeing as how they were her woods, and her darkness, they didn't give Glunda much cause for concern. She had things to do, and woe-betide anyone who messed with a witch when she had business to take care of, especially when the sun was down. They were unlikely to see it come up again.

Heading out across the fields, Glunda made her way over to the Miggins's farm.

The moon was out, but that didn't stop Glunda from stepping in something squishy along the way. *The things I do for people,* she thought, as she tried to pretend it was mud and not something else.

Arriving at the edge of the field she'd watched Alar set on fire, Glunda got out her wand. Taking a moment to check no one was around, she began the spell.

Strictly speaking Glunda was good enough at magic that she didn't need a wand, it was just a piece of wood after all, but she found when working over a large area it helped concentrate the mind. Bringing her thoughts to the singed soil, she imagined it coming to life, every seed cast upon its craggy surface growing higher and taller than you would have thought possible. She used her wand to point to every part of the field, bringing her mind to all four corners so she didn't miss anything.

When she was done, there was a weight to the soil, an abundance of life desperate to spring forth. There was also a great emptiness in the pit of her stomach. Fecunding an entire field always left her more hungry than she had ever felt before. Packing away her wand, Glunda contemplated what she would have to eat when she got home.

Off on the hillside, a light flared in the darkness. Glunda froze. She couldn't see who it was, but judging by the late hour, the pointy hat, and the ethereal light so expertly conjured, if it wasn't Marleena Hearthcrow come to stick her nose in where it was not wanted, Glunda would gladly eat her own hat. She'd obviously seen what Glunda was up to, and had conjured the light so Glunda would see that she'd been seen, but now what? Was she going to come down so that they could have it out there and then? Glunda ate a carrot to build up her strength as she watched the figure cross the hill, climb aboard a broomstick, and fly off into the night, the magical light winking out as it disappeared amongst the stars in the sky.

Glunda threw the remains of her carrot over her shoulder. Clearly tonight's activities were going to come back and bite her in the backside. No good deed goes unpunished. The question was where, and when?

Turns out the where was her place, and the when was the next day, right after breakfast.

Glunda was busy washing up when there was a knock at the door. "Marleena. Do come in. I've been expecting you."

"Have you? How nice."

"Maybe. What can I do for you?"

Marleena Hearthcrow looked concerned. "Are you alright, Glunda? You look tired. Have you been getting enough rest?"

"Spare me, Marleena. I'm not in the mood. Just say your piece and be on your way."

"Very well. We agreed that we would not get involved in this year's harvest, yet there you were last night fecunding one of your neighbour's fields. Care to explain yourself?"

"To you? No. This is my land. I don't have to explain myself to anybody."

"You went against the wishes of the conclave. That cannot go unanswered."

"If I did then I'm not the only one. This entire land is ripe with magic, from one end to the other. I doubt you'll find a fief that hasn't been tampered with in some way or another."

"My fief remains unmolested. Of that I guarantee."

"Yes, but every fief *around* yours has been messed with, hasn't it? And not by the witches who live there, according to them. Coincidence? I think not. Someone's been fecunding all over the place, and not for free I'll bet. Speaking of which, that's a nice shawl you've got there. Is it new?"

Marleena touched the shawl that lay across her shoulders. Its black lacework was very fine indeed. "What, this old thing? I've had it forever. You're not suggesting I went behind the conclave's back just so I could buy a few shawls, are you?"

"I'm not suggesting anything. But I might have to if people start spreading vicious rumours about me."

Marleena Hearthcrow grinned triumphantly. "Well now, the apple has fallen far from the tree. Who would have thought that dear, sweet Glunda would resort to such threats. It seems that being Keeper of the Cauldron is too great a burden for one so young, something we shall have to take into consideration next time around."

"Do as you wish, Marleena. It makes no difference to me."

Marleena Hearthcrow shrugged. She headed for the door. "I shall convey your sentiments to the conclave next time we meet."

"And I shall remind the conclave of a witch's duty."

Marleena paused in the open doorway. She gave Glunda an amused look. "Which is?"

"To help people. Because a happy horse is everybody's horse, or so I've been told."

Mistress Hearthcrow burst out laughing. She tried to think of something to say but every time she did she just started laughing again. Exiting Glunda's hovel, her continued amusement could be heard all the way down the garden path.

Glunda kicked her armchair, stubbing her toe. She sat down to rub her injured foot. Well, that went well, she mused. What should I do next? Set my house on fire?

CHAPTER EIGHT

The weather that summer was magnificent. Long, hot, sunny days made for dips in the river and cooking on an open fire, followed by cool clear nights perfect for sitting and chatting with family and friends over a drink or two. Everyone agreed it was the best summer they'd had in a long time, and whilst it might have been a bit too warm for the crops in the field, a few expertly dug irrigation trenches soon took care of that, so nobody was overly concerned (at least nobody with more than a few summers under their belts that is).

Glunda spent her days wandering the paths of her fief, lending a hand wherever she could. Mistress Hearthcrow's threat to call a conclave had come to nothing, meaning Glunda had been right on the money about who had been doing all the illicit fecunding about the place. Not that she thought she had gotten away with her own rule breaking at all. She fully expected her generosity to come back to bite her at some point, she just wasn't sure how much she would care when it did.

When she wasn't out walking, Glunda was either picnicking with Ellsa Puddleglump or learning to ride with Alayah Buckthorn. Glunda enjoyed Ellsa's company more and more these days. She was surprisingly funny, and she didn't demand too much of Glunda in terms of entertainment in return. In fact, she was often the one with the most stories to tell, being the best place to go to get all the gossip. Ellsa was a good listener, and so people liked to tell her stuff, stuff they probably shouldn't but needed to get off their chest. And like all good listeners when presented with information they didn't really want or need, Ellsa simply smiled and nodded and stored it away for future reference, because you never knew when it might come in handy, especially when it came to helping people out of a sticky situation. She only told Glunda certain things because what good was useful information if you didn't share it with those that needed to know? And Glunda, knowing the power of knowledge, was more than happy to accept. Like Ellsa, she understood that the more you knew the more you could help others (although she did take a certain amount of pleasure in knowing who was messing about with who behind who's back. She was only human after all).

The horse riding Glunda just did for fun. Her friendship with Alayah Buckthorn had really grown that night she'd spent at her camp. For two people born to such different lives, they had a surprising amount in common. When Alayah had discovered Glunda did not know how to ride she had insisted on teaching her, and Glunda had come to love their little fortnightly sessions out on the plains of her fief. Helping people was a good and noble thing to do, but it paid to do something purely for yourself once in a while, otherwise what was the point? You became a slave to life, and such a person was no use to anyone.

It was on a particularly sunny day towards the end of summer, sat atop Picnic Hill, that Glunda first heard of the rumblings among the local farmers. Or at least, amongst the farmers' sons.

"They're not happy, y'know," said Ellsa, as she tackled a particularly large cream cake. "Without the fecund this has been the hardest season most of them have ever known. And there's no telling what'll come up come harvest time. If they don't end up with an abundance of vegetables, they might actually revolt!"

"No one's going to revolt," said Glunda. "They're farmers. They just like to complain about everything."

Glunda and Ellsa were sat looking out over the Miggins's farm, on the same hill they had watched Alar Reave destroy that field all those months ago. It seemed to have been revived, thanks to Glunda's late night shenanigans, but they could tell from here that its yield wasn't as big or bountiful as it should have been.

Ellsa, her cream cake demolished, started sucking the residue off the tips of each one of her fingers. "How do you think the harvest will go? People are talking about prices going up and all sorts."

"I don't know," said Glunda. "Maybe not as good as last year but I'm sure it'll be fine."

Ellsa was less sure, but with nothing to back up her fear but more fears, she kept it to herself for now.

Unfortunately, Ellsa was right. Harvest time came around, and for most of them what came out of the ground would not be winning any prizes any time soon. It didn't help that an outbreak of silver scurf and black scab had turned most of the potato harvest into an unsightly mess, or that the mages' attempts to fix the outbreaks only seemed to have made things worse (not that they would ever admit to such a thing).

When all was said and done, nobody was happy with the way things had turned out, least of all Clum and his mates, since they were the ones who had done most of the work.

Clum and his father rode their cartload of vegetables up to the gates of the mages' castle. Clum was dispatched with a nod of the head to go knock on its closed door, then they sat and waited in angry silence for someone to answer.

"Say what you like about the witches," Clum's father grumbled, "at least they had the decency to come get their vegetables themselves."

Clum said nothing, even though there was plenty he *could* say about *a lot* of people, some of whom weren't sitting a million miles away from him at that very moment.

Eventually the gates swung open and a young boy gestured them forward into the castle's outer courtyard.

As they climbed down from their wagon, a mage in gold-embroidered, food-stained robes waddled over, a half-eaten turkey leg in hand. He had a nervous looking Alar Reave in tow. "Ah, Mr Miggins," boomed the mage. "Good to see you again."

Clum's father almost tugged his forelock, until he remembered he didn't like being called mister. "Lor... *Mister* Feffle. How are you, sir?"

The mage eyed the farmer. "Very well, thank you. And you? How's the wife? Mayve, is it?"

"Still dead, sir. Going on three years now. But my boy Clum is doing well for himself, thanks for asking."

Lord Feffle stopped chewing on his mouthful of food and swallowed loudly. "Yes, well... Good to know, eh. Um, let's have a look at what we've got, shall we." He hurried round the back of the cart. Throwing back the canvas cover, he inspected the vegetables beneath. "Hmm... Now let's see." Clum and his father exchanged a knowing look. "They look a bit... small, don't you think?"

"They are as they came out of the ground, my lord."

"Yes but, normally they're a lot..."—Lord Feffle waved his hands about expansively—"bigger."

Clum snorted. "Yeah, well, if you lot had done a better job of blessing the land, they would have been a lot"—Clum mockingly mimicked Lord Feffle's expansive hand waving—"bigger."

The two men looked at the boy reproachfully. "Nevertheless," said Lord Feffle, "I'm not sure we can pay the usual price for such goods. We wouldn't want to be taken for a ride."

Clem Miggins glared at his son. "How much did you have in mind, my lord?"

The mage considered the consignment once more. "I'd say... fifty. Maybe fifty-five."

"For what?" said Clum.

"For all of it."

"All of it! But it's worth three times that, and you know it. This is a fix! I can't believe you can stand there and look us in the eye, and—"

Clum's father stepped forward, getting between Clum and the mage before his boy did something he might regret. He was no less angry, but he knew getting angry wasn't going to get them anywhere. "What my son is trying to say, my lord, is fifty-five gold pieces—"

"Fifty," said Lord Feffle coldly.

Clum's father fought down the rage. "Fifty gold pieces is barely enough for us to restock on seed. It's certainly not enough for us to turn any kind of a profit. If you could see your way to seventy, say, or even seventy-five, I'm sure we could do you a good price on next year's crop as well."

Alar Reave stepped forward. "That sounds perfectly reasonable, wouldn't you say, my lord? I'm sure we could—" He was stopped by a raised finger and a stern look from Lord Feffle.

"I'm sorry but that's the best we can do. Times are tough, as you know. We're all having to cut back where we can. But you're welcome to take your vegetables and try and get a better price for them elsewhere. I heard the Marsh Lands are crying out for carrots and cucumbers this time of year."

"A caravan? Through bandit country? We'd never survive the trip."

"On the contrary, if you were to take a mage along for protection your survival is almost guaranteed."

Clem Miggins squinted at the head mage. "Oh yes, and how much is that gonna cost me?"

Lord Feffle grinned wolfishly. "Fifty gold pieces."

Clum and his father rode their empty cart out of the castle. Behind them, a beaming Lord Feffle stood next to a pile of ludicrously cheap vegetables.

"Forgive me for saying, sir, but that was a little harsh, don't you think?" said Lord Reave. "Farmer Miggins still has to make a living, you know."

"And that he has. I offered no less than what I consider to be fair market value. Whether he took it or not was entirely up to him."

Easy to say when you're the one with all the money, thought Alar. "I just think we could have been a bit... fairer."

Lord Feffle laughed. "Whoever told you life was fair, Lord Reave? Where is that written?" He burped loudly. "Now, sort this lot out, would you. I have matters to attend to. Keep the good stuff and sling the rest on the compost heap."

"We're not going to keep it all?"

"Certainly not. What kind of a person eats vegetables all the time?"

"But why buy it in the first place if we're not going to eat it?"

"To keep it out of the witches' hands, of course. Why else? If we have it, they don't, and if they don't have any vegetables they cannot threaten our position as Guardians of the Golden Key now, can they? Goodness, Lord Reave, I can see we're going to have to work on your people skills. You clearly still have a lot to learn."

"So what did you do?" said Shaymus.

"What else could I do? I took the fifty and went on my way," said Clum's father, finishing his drink in one long, furious gulp. "Bloody mages." He slammed his tankard down on the bar, the barman filling it without being asked. A good barman knows the mood of the pub, and the mood in The Ploughed Furrow that night was one of heavy hearts and even heavier drinking.

The farmers were gathered at the bar, close to the booze. Their boys were at a table in the corner, a flagon of ale each and a few more besides for when they started to run out. They wanted to limit their visits to the bar as much as possible. None of them were very happy with any of their 'old gits' at the moment.

Clum and Jayce were there, along with Eli and the Curtiss twins. Jayce was doing most of the talking, and most of the drinking, which kind of went hand in hand. "So they stiffed you on the price?"

"Yup," said Clum.

Jayce used a phrase that would have got him a clip round the ear if his mother had heard him. "Reckon they'll do the same to us?"

"I wouldn't be surprised."

"What if we took our goods up to town? Reckon we'd get a better price there?"

"You might, but I doubt it. No one's got any money these days. If the mages won't pony up, I don't see why anyone else will."

"Damn it," Jayce growled into his drink. "I tell you what, it's about time these mages were taken down a peg or two.

What do you reckon?" Eli and the two Curtiss boys all nodded ominously.

Clum didn't like where this was headed. "What about the witches?"

"What about 'em?"

"I dunno. Maybe they can help. Talk to the mages, something like that?"

"Hah! I wouldn't count on it. One lot's as bad as the other, far as I can tell."

"It don't hurt to ask, does it?"

"That's up to you, mate," said Jayce, sloshing about a flagon of ale. "But I can't see them mages giving up nothing without a fight. One way or another, it'll be up to us to 'elp persuade 'em I reckon."

Nodding their collective heads, the table growled enthusiastically.

CHAPTER NINE

C lum arrived at Glunda's house with a loaf of bread under his arm. He had a vague idea that you should arrive with a gift when you've come to ask someone a favour, but he felt strange bringing a witch flowers, and he didn't have the money for anything else, so bread it was. To be fair it was a nice loaf, a harvest bloomer, all crusty on the outside and fluffy within, but at the end of the day it was still just a loaf of bread. Whether it did the trick depended on how Glunda felt about baked goods, Clum supposed.

"Clum! What a pleasant surprise. Do come in."

"Hello, Glunda. I, um, brought you this."

"A loaf of bread! How wonderful." Glunda sniffed her gift with great joy. "Smells amazing. Let's have some now whilst it's still warm. I have some butter on the windowsill that will go with this a treat!"

Clum and Glunda sat on Glunda's doorstep eating bread and butter and listening to the birds sing. Having turned her garden into a vegetable patch, there was nowhere else for them to sit.

"Your taters have come up nice," said Clum, turning bright red when he realised that could be taken the wrong way by some women.

Glunda appeared not to notice. "Yes, they have, haven't they? I can't wait to pull them up, see what lies beneath. Speaking of which, how are things down on the farm? How's this year's harvest looking?"

"Oh, alright. It's been better. Actually, that's kind of what I wanted to talk to you about. See, the mages have been buying up everything they can, only they've been paying half what they're worth coz they know we ain't got no one else to sell to, since everyone's being a bit skint and that. There's talk of a caravan but that doesn't look likely, what with all the bandits between here and there."

Glunda understood at once. Providing protection was the mages' responsibility, their 'blessing of the land' which they did in return for being in charge for six months of the year. But since they were in charge all the time now it seemed they were no longer willing to do their sworn duty. "How much are they charging to provide safe passage?"

"Too much. We can't afford it, no one can, so we're stuck selling to the Drupe Mages whether we like it or not."

"I'm sorry to hear that, Clum, but what can I do? I don't have the money to buy your vegetables, and the witches don't have the right kind of magic to protect you against bandits and the like."

"I dunno. Could we not go back to the way things were? Things were alright then. If you was to get the key back from the Drupe Mages you could bless the land and have your Offering again, same as before. You wouldn't have to grow your own vegetables or nuthin'. And the farmers would be behind you on that, I know they would!"

Glunda shook her head. "If we tried to get the key from the Drupe Mages it could mean war, and I don't think the other witches would be willing to risk that, even if the people were behind us."

"But you could ask, couldn't you? Ask them if they'd be willing to help?"

The pleading in Clum's eyes was like a thousand puppies begging for a treat. It was almost unbearable. "Yes, Clum," said Glunda finally. "I could ask."

A conclave was called for later that day. Its purpose was kept secret, for fear of the Drupe Mages getting wind of their plans, so of course every witch who arrived knew exactly why they were there already. Witches, being a nosey bunch, were excellent at keeping secrets, especially when they were someone else's.

Mistress Hearthcrow arrived an hour early, ready to put the kibosh on this idea of theirs before it had a chance to take root, only to find Glunda and her little cohort of young witches sitting waiting for the conclave to begin. Opposite them sat a handful of elder witches all looking a bit glum, probably because there was no booze anywhere in sight.

"I hope you haven't started without me. That would be rather rude."

"Not at all, Mistress Hearthcrow. We're just waiting for everyone to arrive. Please, have a seat."

Mistress Hearthcrow spotted Clum sitting off to the side, behind Glunda. "What is *he* doing here? This is a conclave for witches."

"He is here at my request, and as the Keeper of the Cauldron it is up to me how the conclave is run, not you."

"You won't be Keeper of the Cauldron for much longer, you know. The equinox is almost upon us."

"Nevertheless, I am Keeper of the Cauldron now. So please take your seat and be quiet, Mistress Hearthcrow."

Amidst a flurry of surprised looks and elbowed giggles from both sides of the conclave, Marleena Hearthcrow reluctantly did as she was told.

The conclave sat in silence as they waited for the last of their number to arrive. There was a disturbing unity amongst the young witches, a collective sense of purpose that Mistress Hearthcrow didn't like one bit. She tried engaging her side in conversation but none of them were interested. For the most part they just wanted to get the conclave over with and go home.

As the last witch took her seat, Glunda called the meeting to order.

"Ladies, I have called you all here to discuss the Drupe Mages and their unprecedented seizure of power. The last year of them being in charge has been disastrous for the people. Crop yields are down, coffers are empty, and the coming year looks to be more difficult yet, with no money for seed and a land exhausted by the lack of a proper blessing." A handful of witches, the ones Glunda suspected of performing blessings behind everyone's backs, shifted guiltily in their seats. "The Drupe Mages cannot be allowed to continue as they have. We must get back the key and return to the way things were before it is too late."

"Ha! Easy enough for you to say when you were the one lost us the key in the first place."

"And you think you'd have done any better, Ismay Silverbirch? On your own, in the lion's den?" The elder witch looked suitably embarrassed. "I admit, the loss of the key was my fault. I was unprepared for what happened. But if we were to present a united front, if we were to stand together before the Mage Council, I am sure we could make them see the error of their ways."

"But it's not just them, is it?" said Marleena Hearthcrow. "It's his lot as well. The Drupe Mages never would have done what they did if they didn't think the people were behind them every step of the way."

Glunda glanced at Clum, who reluctantly rose to his feet. "You're right. The farmers did side with the Drupe Mages. They were fed a pack of lies and they swallowed them hook, line, and sinker. But I've spoken with my mates and there are enough of us now who see the Drupe Mages for what they really are. If you were to stand up to them, you'd have our backing, I guarantee it."

"And you speak for all farmers, do you?"

"Not all of them, no. But I speak for enough. They're not happy with the way things are heading. They just want to go back to the way things were."

Surprisingly, the idea seemed to meet with the approval of many of the elder witches, judging by the looks on their faces. Lucrative though it may have been, the past year had been hard work for all of them, especially the ones who had grown accustomed to hefty lunches followed by long afternoon naps. They weren't about to turn down a bit of status quo if it was on offer.

Marleena Hearthcrow, who had done better than most, had to act fast. "I don't know about that," she said. "Most of us have done quite well for ourselves this winter, including yourself, Glunda. I'm not sure we'd be willing to give that up."

"Speak for yourself," scoffed Jemima Oakenleaf. "I've bin working my ass off making potions and unguents for every sniff and snivel for miles around. It's bin a right pain. If there's even half a chance we could go back tae the way things were I say we jump at it."

"Maybe, but there should be some kind of... recompense, don't you think? A little something for our ongoing pain and suffering?"

"What? Och, aye. I do indeed. A little recompense to, um, grease the wheels, like. For all the, er, pain and suffering and that."

"What sort of recompense?" said Glunda grimly.

Marleena Hearthcrow considered for a while. "An increase in the Offering should suffice. A few more vegetables each year, say, or perhaps even a coin or two?"

Glunda looked to Clum who shrugged helplessly. "That may be possible," she said. "We would have to see what the farmers have to say on the matter. But for now, do I have your permission to try and broker a deal with the Drupe Mages? Will you back said deal, if one can be made?"

Jemima Oakenleaf laughed. "Lass, you put a bit of coin in my pocket and I'll back any deal you like."

CHAPTER TEN

Glunda went around her already perfectly clean hovel dusting and tidying up. She fluffed a cushion, bashed it angrily into a misshapen lump, then, with a sigh, fluffed it back into cushiony perfection once more. She hated that she was going to so much trouble to impress a Drupe Mage, and Alar Reave no less, but she was aware that if you wanted someone to do you a favour you had to be nice to them, even if you did sometimes feel like using their face to practise your cushion fluffing technique.

There was a knock at the door. Taking a couple of deep breaths, Glunda went to answer it, plastering on her best fake smile along the way. "Alar! How wonderful to see you. Welcome to my humble home."

"Er... Hello, Glunda," said Alar warily. "Is everything alright? Not too early, am I?"

"Not at all, not at all. Please, do come in. Have a seat, won't you? Would you like some tea?"

Glunda had brought the little table down from upstairs. It sat between the two armchairs drenched in an over-sized tablecloth, a myriad of cakes and biscuits jammed in amongst her mother's best china and an unfortunate teapot that was shaped like a goose which she never normally used. Alar eyed the effort with a certain amount of hard-won trepidation. "Yes, thank you. Some tea would be nice."

"Excellent, excellent. Well, don't stand on ceremony, will you. Please, do sit down."

Alar sank into one of the chairs, watching as Glunda bustled about making her guest some tea. She didn't seem to know where to start, reaching first for the pot then the milk. She automatically put sugar in his before remembering to check if that was correct — "One sugar is fine, thank you, Glunda." — and her attempts to cram half a dozen biscuits onto the saucer were confusing at best. Eventually Alar couldn't stand it any longer. "Glunda, whatever's going on I wish you would just sit down and tell me. We've known each other long enough to speak plainly to one another."

Glunda looked at the confusion of cake before her. "Yes, you're right, of course. Thank you, Alar." Putting everything down, she placed herself in the chair opposite, tossing its cushion onto the floor behind her. Placing her hands in her lap, she gathered her thoughts. "What it is, is this: the harvest this year has been bad. Not 'struggling through the winter' bad, but bad enough that next year could be a real problem."

"You can't blame us for that. I came to you when—"

Glunda stopped him with a raised hand. "That's not what this is about. We want to fix the problem, not the blame. So, with that in mind, I'd like to discuss going back to the way things were, with the Drupe Mages being in charge in spring and summer, and the witches running things during the autumn and winter time. We think it might be best all round, and I can tell you that most of the farmers hereabouts agree."

"You took this to them first?"

"No, they came to us. This is their idea. I'm just the one putting it to you."

"I see." Alar took a sip of tea. "So, tell me something, if this is about the harvest why don't you simply do what you did before? You bless the land like you used to do and everything would be fine, wouldn't it?"

Glunda shifted uncomfortably in her seat. "It's not as simple as that. If we were to do as you say, there are some of us who… I mean, some of the older witches, they're not the sort who… Oh, hells bells, they just won't do it, alright. They'd see that as being pushed around by the Drupe Mages, and they won't allow that to happen, no matter what. Some of them remember what it was like before the agreement, and they won't let that happen again."

"Let what happen?"

"I don't know. But if you ask them about it they get pretty mad so it can't have been good." Glunda let out a frustrated sigh. "So what do you say? Do you think the Drupe Mages would be willing to go back to the way things were? For the good of the people?"

"For the good of the people?" scoffed Alar. "Don't make me laugh. You could help the people if you wanted to. This has got nothing to do with them. This is about the witches and their insane need to tell everyone what to do all the time. Don't try and deny it. You lot love lording it over people, acting all smug like you know everything. And now you're not getting the respect you so *richly* deserve you're acting like we're the bad guys. I'm sorry, Glunda, but that's an insult to the pair of us and you know it."

"I know nothing of the sort. And I resent the implication, Lord Reave. You want to be in charge, fine. But you're the ones responsible for the bad harvest, and don't think the people don't know that."

"I think the people know *exactly* whose fault it is," said Alar loudly.

"As do I!" Glunda replied.

The two glared at each other over the mess of tea and biscuits. With great deliberation, Alar put down his cup and saucer. "I think it's about time I was going."

"Yes," said Glunda icily, "I think it is."

Alar Reave marched down the isolated country lane, high hawthorn hedgerows either side of him. Who the hell does she think she is? he raged, acting like this was all our fault! I mean, yes, the mage's attempts at blessing the land hadn't gone according to plan, and yes, Lord Feffle had been a little. .. robust in his dealings with the local farmers, but the witches could have helped if they'd wanted to. Blessed the land, increased the harvest, that sort of thing? More vegetables meant more money after all. The truth was they *chose* not to help, meaning some of this mess was at least partly their fault. And the people would be able to see that, wouldn't they? Even if those damn veg witches could not.

Alar spotted two figures on the road ahead, coming towards him. A couple of farm boys by the look of them, a little worse for drink judging by the way they staggered down the road. As they got nearer, he tried to remember their names. He didn't know much, but he knew they didn't like to be called 'Boy', not to their face at least.

"Good afternoon, Jayce. And, er, Eli, is it? Forgive me. My memory is not the best."

"Well look who it isn't," Jayce slurred. "Lord Reave, as I live and breathe. Greetings, my lord. An honour to make your acquaintance." Whipping off his hat, Jayce bent low in a dramatic bow, his friend watching on with a malicious look in his eye.

"Please, there's no need for—"

"Tell me, *my lord*," Jayce continued, "are you enjoying all those vegetables you've been buying? I hope so. Not that you couldn't afford a nice bit of meat to go with 'em, the price you've been paying."

Alar took a half step back. "I think perhaps you've been at the ale, Jayce. Perhaps you should head home and sleep it off."

Jayce and Eli moved to surround Alar. "An' I fink me and Eli don't care what some mage finks, do we, Eli? So wot you got to say about *that*, my lord?"

"I say that—" Alar ducked as Jayce lunged at him, his fist flying over Alar's head. He grabbed for some dried fruit in his pocket but lost hold when Eli kicked him in the back, sending him sprawling. He rolled over in time to see Jayce bearing down on him. Kicking him in the knee, Alar flung a handful of dirt in Eli's face. Stumbling back, Eli fell over his friend and the two of them collapsed into a drunken heap.

Scrambling to his feet, Alar ran off down the road, the two farm boys flinging rocks and insults after him until he was well out of reach. Alar didn't slow until he was sure he'd left them both far behind, and even then he walked briskly until he was back behind the castle walls once more.

In the courtyard, Alar had the misfortune of running into Lord Feffle, who had just got back from his daily constitutional. "Is this how we go out in public, Lord Reave? With mud on our robes and... What is that on your face? Is that blood?"

Alar touched his cheek and his hand came away wet. Damn it. He must have cut his face when he fell. "Yes, sir. I'm sorry. I had a run in with a couple of local lads."

Lord Feffle chuckled. "Been romancing their sweetheart no doubt. Happens to the best of us. Just be more discreet next time. We have a reputation to uphold after all."

"No, sir, it wasn't anything like that. It was..." Oh to hell with it! Alar couldn't pretend anymore. "It was to do with the harvest, sir, and the low prices we have been forcing on the people. They can't make a living, sir, and they blame us, which frankly isn't surprising. What *is* surprising is how little you seem to care. We are causing real hardship for these people, and despite being in a position to do something about it we don't, which I don't understand. Are we not meant to help people? Isn't that why we sought power in the first place?"

Lord Feffle laughed a laugh of genuine amusement. He patted Lord Reave on the shoulder. "Goodness, they really did put the wind up you, didn't they? Help people indeed. It is for people to help themselves, Lord Reave, always has been. Do you think if we were in dire straits the villagers would be lining up at our door to help us? Of course not. We are alone in this world, and all there is is what you take for yourself, and what you are willing to do to get it. Nothing else."

Alar shook his head. It was a waste of time, but he'd try anyway. "The witches want to go back to the way things were. The farmers too. They want us to hand over the Golden Key, and I'm starting to think it might not be bad idea. Let them take the blame for a while. I'm quite sure I've had enough of it for now."

Lord Feffle gave Alar a pitying look. "You've had an ordeal, Lord Reave. Go get yourself cleaned up, and we'll have no more of this key nonsense. Despite what you think, it is best that we are in charge, and I intend to keep it that way no matter what the witches, or the townsfolk, or anyone else may think."

Alar's head dropped. He couldn't remember ever having been this tired. "As you wish, my lord."

Lord Feffle patted him on the back. Stuffing his hands in his pockets, he walked away whistling a happy tune.

Glunda approached Picnic Hill with a carrot in hand. She'd already had a large helping of casserole before leaving the house, but when you got a note inviting you to a secret late-night assignation in a remote spot it paid to come prepared.

Glunda made her way to the top of the hill. It was eerily quiet, with a chill wind that somehow found its way down the back of her neck. Whoever she was here to meet she hoped they made themselves known pretty soon. She did not want to hang around any longer than was absolutely necessary.

"Hello, Glunda," said Alar, stepping out from behind a bush.

Glunda bit back the spell that sprang to her lips. "Alar! What's going on? Why are we meeting here like this?"

"I did not wish to be seen, for both our sakes. I'm sure you understand."

"I'm sure I don't. Who are you hiding from? For what— Who's that?!"

"It's Clum," said Alar. "I asked him to come as well."

Clum trudged his way to the top of the hill. He looked at the mage and the witch curiously. "I got a note," he said.

"That was from me," said Alar. "I wanted to speak to you both about everything that's been going on. Glunda said that the people wanted to go back to the way things were. Is that true?"

Clum kind of shrugged. "Yeah, I guess."

"Only, I might have a way we could do that. What if we agreed amongst ourselves, unofficially of course, that the witches were in charge during autumn and winter? They could bless the land as before, then when it came time to harvest, you'd have a decent yield to sell on at market, which should get you a better price all round."

"Yeah, after the witches take their cut," mumbled Clum.

"And what about the key?" said Glunda. "Who keeps that?"

"We would have to keep the key, I'm afraid. Lord Feffle would not be willing to give that up."

"So we'd be working for you! Is that how it is? The witches do all the work and the Drupe Mages take all the glory! Are you kidding me? Did you really think we would agree to something like that?"

"I'm trying to think of something that is best for everyone. The people need help, and you are best placed to give it. But we cannot give up the key. The Mage Council would never agree to such a thing."

"And the conclave would never agree to such a humiliation. I can't believe you would suggest such a thing. I thought you were smarter than that, Alar. No, I'm sorry, but without the key there is no deal."

"You cannot have the key, Glunda."

"Then no deal, Alar!"

"Oh, for crying out loud, stop it! Just stop it, the pair of you!"

Glunda and Alar regarded Clum in surprise. Standing with his fists clenched, he shook with rage, his face a twisted mask of fury. Neither of them had ever seen him like that before. For a moment, Alar thought he was about to get another thumping.

"Don't you see what's going on? Whilst you two bicker over who gets to run what, people are going hungry! You're so caught up in your own little struggle for glory you forget about those you're actually meant to help. We suffer whilst you do nothing, blaming each other for the mess you've both made. The key, the key, who cares about the key?! The people need help and all you care about is some damn key? Honestly, I think we'd be better off if we got shot of the whole lot of ya!"

Glunda and Alar exchanged a guilty look. He was right of course. When there was food on the table did it matter who put it there? Not to the hungry. And feeding the hungry should be glory enough. A wise person didn't need an award to know they had done the right thing. As Alayah might say, a happy herd was a joy to all.

Glunda went over and took Clum's hand. He looked fearful of what she might do, but she simply smiled at him warmly. "I think I have a solution, but it won't be easy. I'm going to need help." She turned to Alar. "From both of you."

Alar looked sceptical. "I'm listening," he said dubiously.

CHAPTER ELEVEN

I t was the day before the autumn equinox, a mere two days after the secret meeting on Picnic Hill. Alar Reave came down to breakfast to find the other mages in a jolly mood. Something had tickled them no end it seemed.

"Lord Reave!" barked Lord Cundalunn, a loud and obnoxious mage not known for his love of levity. "Come take a look at this. Have you ever seen such a thing?" Lord Cundalunn shoved a piece of yellow paper into Alar's hand. It was an announcement, inviting people to a meeting that night to discuss the formation of a new Council of the People, 'For the management of affairs of the realm for the betterment of all'. Lord Cundalunn jabbed at the notice, a look of sheer joy on his craggy face. "They want to have elections and everything! Can you believe that? As if we would ever allow such a thing."

"I don't know, Lord Cundalunn. It looks like they've put some thought into this. We might want to take them more seriously."

"Pah! And pigs might fly!"

This suggestion prompted a lot of oinking and flapping of hands from the surrounding mages. Clearly they thought the whole thing was some hilarious joke.

Lord Feffle entered, clutching a yellow notice of his own. Unlike the rest, he wasn't smiling. "Have you seen this?" he demanded.

"Oh yes, my lord." Lord Cundalunn chuckled. "Most amusing."

"Amusing? You think this is funny?!"

The laughter stopped suddenly. "Isn't it?" Lord Cundalunn squeaked.

"Are you mad! What do you think would happen if the peasants decided they didn't need us to boss them around anymore? Do you know how many of them there are? They breed like rabbits! If they decide to do away with us and start thinking for themselves do you really think there is anything we can do to stop them?"

The mages stared at each other in bemused silence, as their entire world came tumbling down around them.

"We must stop this nonsense," continued Lord Feffle. "Nip it in the bud. If anyone's got any clever ideas now would be the time."

No one said a thing. For a group who considered themselves smarter than most, it seemed clever ideas were hard to come by. Finally, Alar Reave took a step forward. "If I may, my lord, I'd say that it is already too late to stop the meeting. Word must be out by now. I'd suggest instead that we go along and present our case for keeping things as they are. And, should that fail, make sure that we are the ones on this council of theirs, and not those that might wish to do us harm."

The gathered mages nodded their approval. They all knew who he meant by 'those who might wish to do us harm'.

"Good idea, Lord Reave. We will all go. A collective show of force. Let them see what they are up against. Make the arrangements, would you."

"Of course, my lord."

Breakfast continued, albeit in a more subdued manner. At the far end of the table, opposite Lord Reave, one of the elder mages picked up the yellow leaflet and considered it for a moment. "Where did this come from anyhow? How did it get inside the castle? Anybody know?"

Alar shrugged. "No idea. One of the servants must have brought it in I suppose."

Clum and his father rode their cart into town for the morning market, Clum half asleep on the bench next to his dad. He yawned loudly.

"You were out late last night," his father said. "A girl, is it?"

"Um, something like that. Yeah."

"Good lad. No point going through life on your own, eh. They can be a right pain sometimes, but having a wife certainly gives you something to do alright."

Clum didn't know what to say to that.

They passed a line of trees next to the road, each with a yellow piece of paper pinned to it. After they passed the third one, Clum's father's curiosity got the better of him. "'A Council of the People'? What the hell's that when it's at home? Do you know anything about this?"

"I heard something about it, yeah. People reckon that if we ran things, instead of a bunch of posh know-it-alls, we could do what was best for everyone."

"Yeah, best for them that runs things and nobody else you mean. Whose idea was this?"

"Um... Jayce's dad, I think."

"Shaymus Padeen? That idiot! And I suppose he plans on nominating himself to be in charge of it all?"

"I think he did say something about that, yes."

"I'll bet he did, the greedy, no good, self-serving little swine! Well, we'll see about his little plan, don't you worry. If anyone's going to run things around here it'll be me!" Clem glanced at his son. "For the, er, betterment of all, of course."

"Of course, Dad," said Clum, in as flat a tone as possible. "Good idea."

Glunda was awoken by a loud banging on her door. She clumped down her narrow hall, yawning as she pulled her dressing gown lazily around her tired body. "Who is it?" she called through the closed door, because not just anyone should see a witch in her dressing gown.

"It's Marleena Hearthcrow. Open up. I need to talk to you."

Glunda pulled open the door and Mistress Hearthcrow barged her way inside. She was clutching a crumpled piece of yellow paper. "Have you seen this?"

"Obviously not, since I have clearly just got out of bed. What is it?"

"Here. Have a read."

Glunda pretended to focus on the words as if it was the first time she had seen them. "A council, eh? Well, good for them. About time they stopped letting the Drupe Mages push them around all the time."

"Good for them? Are you serious? What about us, what are we meant to do? Take orders from a bunch of peasants?"

Glunda wandered into the kitchen to make herself a cup of tea, hotly pursued by Mistress Hearthcrow. She wasn't actually that thirsty, but she didn't want Marleena spotting the stack of yellow leaflets that she had foolishly left sticking out from underneath a chair cushion. "I wouldn't worry about it. I'm sure it'll be fine."

"Well I'm not! This could be the end of us. No more respect, no more authority, no more..."

Cheeky backhanders, thought Glunda. She yawned dramatically to show just how unbothered she was. "Look, if you're that concerned why not go along to the meeting tonight, state your case. Maybe, if there's going to be a council, we should be the ones to run it. We are part of the people after all."

Marleena Hearthcrow froze, her mind suddenly working overtime. "Yes, you're right. Good idea, Glunda. *We* should run the council, not some bunch of uneducated peasants. It'll take some working out but I'm sure we can swing it. We just need to make sure we have enough votes."

"Sounds good. I'll leave that in your capable hands. Now, if you don't mind, I have things to do, the first of which being to have a bath. And much as I enjoy your company, Mistress Hearthcrow, that is one thing I prefer to do alone."

The Corn Exchange was by far the largest building in Wellety Vale. All black wooden beams and white-washed wattle and daub, with a thatched yellow roof and a multitude of leaded windows, it held pride of place at the centre of town, right next to Market Square, a constant reminder to all around that the main business of the local people was growing stuff and selling stuff, usually in that order. It was also where they held all the big dances, which explained how someone had been able to erect a large stage at one end of the massive auction room. Stages weren't the sort of thing you usually had lying around. Where they'd got all the chairs from was another matter, although rumour had it that every pub and tearoom for miles around had found themselves to be 'standing room only' for the day, whether they liked it or not. The chairs had been set out in semi-circled rows facing the stage, with a walkway down the middle should anyone feel the need to make a mad dash for the loo.

Market Square was full of carts by the time Clum and his father arrived. If the Exchange wasn't full already it soon would be. "Damn it," cursed Clum's father. "Look at them all! I'm telling you now, boy, if I miss this meeting there's gonna be hell to pay."

"Why don't you run inside, grab us a couple of seats?" said Clum calmly. "I'll find somewhere to park the cart."

"Good idea, lad," said his father, handing Clum the reins. "You're not as daft as you are cabbage lookin' after all."

Clum watched his father hurry across the square, then, turning the cart around, he rode it out of town along the road that led to the mage's castle.

Clem Miggins barged his way through the slow-moving crowd into the auction room. It was indeed pretty full, and it wasn't just the townspeople who were there either. The witches had staked themselves out a spot to the left of the stage, whilst the mages had taken up most of the chairs to the extreme right, keeping as much distance between themselves and the women in pointy hats as possible. This was probably for the best as who knew what would happen if the two groups got within spitting distance of each other. Not that the attending peasants had anything to worry about. They outnumbered the magic users by at least ten to one, and with more of them arriving by the second it'd be a brave witch or mage who tried to take that lot on without a carefully thought out escape plan in their back pocket.

Spotting a seat at the front of the room, Clem rushed to get himself a decent view.

There were nine seats on the stage, he noticed, five along the middle with two each side bent in at an angle. Who were they for? he wondered. Come to think of it, who was running this thing? There seemed to be a lot of people eager for the meeting to start, and very few people willing to step forward to kick things off.

At the front of the pack of mages, Lord Feffle elbowed Lord Cundalunn in the ribs. "Where's Lord Reave? Coming here was his idea. Why isn't he here..."—Lord Feffle gesticulated wildly—"...sorting things out?"

"He said he had something to attend to at the castle, my lord, but that he would be along shortly."

"Well he better be. I don't like the look of those witches. I think they're up to something."

On the other side of the room, the witches were too busy trying to tap a keg to care what the mages were up to. All except for Mistress Hearthcrow, who was starting to wonder where Glunda was. As Keeper of the Cauldron (whatever that meant on the last day of summer after the year they'd had) she should have been there, helping the witches present a united front. Then again, perhaps it was best she wasn't there. Nothing says 'I'm the one in charge' like nobody stepping up to challenge your authority.

With a decisive nod, Marleena Hearthcrow rose. The noise level in the room dropped as half the audience turned to look. She smiled. Perfect. Making her way onto the stage, she waved the attending crowd into silence.

"Good evening, everyone, and welcome." She paused for dramatic effect. "Today is an auspicious day, the forming of a council to reflect the will of the people and to guide them to a better tomorrow. And I, for one, think it is long past due. Who better to know what is best for the people but the people themselves? It just makes sense. But..."—another dramatic pause—"knowing what is best can be quite difficult. There are a great many things to consider. With that in mind, I should like to offer my services to the council as a sort of... sounding board. A guide, if you will. To help ensure they do not make any mistakes they might later come to regret. We witches do, after all, have a great deal of experience in—"

"Hold up, hold up. Wait one minute." Lord Feffle hurried onto the stage. "Let's not get ahead of ourselves, shall we? There needs to be some discussion first about whether a Council of the People is the right way to go. After all, the Mage Council has been taking care of everyone for generations. Surely we are best placed to guide the people forward to a greater and more abundant prosperity?"

"Hah! Guide yourself to more gold you mean," said Mistress Heathcrow. "We all know what you mages care about most, and it isn't the people."

"Like you're any better! We've all seen what happens when you don't keep the witches happy. Or what doesn't happen, more like. Unless you're willing to pay, that is." Lord Feffle rubbed his fingers together in the universally accepted sign for cash money. "Oh yes, you witches have shown your true colours this year and no mistake!"

"That is outrageous! How *dare* you make such an accusation. We witches have—"

"Oh for crying out loud!" yelled Clem Miggins, leaping to his feet. "Will you two shut up? This is meant to be a council for the people, not just another way for you lot to line your pockets. Honestly, between you witches taking a cut of our crop and you mages paying us pittance for the rest it's a wonder any of us has anything left! Why you think you should get to decide *anything* is beyond me. What are you even doing up there anyhow? Where's Shaymus Padeen? He's the one supposed to be running this thing. Where you at, Shaymus? Get up here and sort this lot out will ya."

Everyone turned to the back of the room, where Shaymus Padeen stood eating a cheese and pickle sandwich. He looked in confusion at the sea of expectant faces staring back at him. "Me?" he said with a mouth full of sandwich. "What's it got to do with me?"

"Well, you're the one called the meeting, aren't ya?"

Shaymus swallowed his half-chewed sandwich with an uncomfortable grimace. "Nowt to do with me," he managed. "Must be some other Shaymus or something."

With perfect timing, the doors of the auction room burst open to reveal Glunda Ashwillow, all steely-eyed and determined, with an equally determined Alar Reave and Clum Miggins either side of her.

"He didn't call the meeting, we did," said Glunda loudly.

A murmur ran through the crowd as Glunda, Alar, and Clum marched up the centre aisle and onto the stage. "Thank you, Mistress Hearthcrow," said Glunda. "I can take it from here."

The elder witch knew better than to argue, as did Lord Feffle, who had already quietly slipped off the stage rather than go through the humiliation of being dismissed by one of his juniors.

Glunda went to the front of the stage, where she waited patiently for the shock and speculation to die down. Only when it was properly quiet did she begin to speak.

"What a year, eh?" A few people chuckled. "Can't say I've ever seen one like it, or that I want to see another one like it ever again. You know, I used to think that being a witch was about helping people no matter what, but it turns out that when the 'what' hits the fan that soon goes out the window in favour of helping yourself and sod everybody else."

A few of the elder witches looked like they wanted to protest, but when they saw some of the looks they were getting from some of the locals they thought better of it. Some of the mages grinned at that, until they spotted Alar glaring down at them. "I wouldn't look so smug if I were you. It's not like we've made a great pretence of helping anyone else out either."

Glunda continued, "It is clear to me now that putting power into the hands of the wealthy few is a mistake, but thankfully it is a mistake that we can do something about. So, to that end, Alar, Clum, and I propose forming a Council of the People, a group of nine elected officials who can make decisions on the people's behalf, made up of five laypeople, two witches, and two mages, all of whom would work together for the benefit of all."

"Hold on," said Clum's father, "what's with all the witches and mages? Why do they get to be on the council?"

"Because they too are part of this community," said Glunda.

"But what's to stop them taking over like they did before?"

"The fact that there's four of them and five of us, Dad," said Clum. "Now sit down and let Glunda speak, will you!"

In a state of shock at his son finally standing up for himself, Clem Miggins sat back down.

"The main job of the council," said Glunda, "will be to decide on a fair price for fruits and vegetables, and a fair exchange rate for the blessing of the land and the protection of its people from bandits and the like. No longer will one group take advantage of another because they have what the other side needs most."

Lord Feffle burst out laughing. Shaking his head, he rose to his feet. "Do what you like, young lady. The Drupe Mages will have no part of it. We have all the fruit that we could possibly need, meaning there is nothing we want that we can't take for ourselves. Why you think we would submit to the rulings of some council is beyond me." He started heading for the door.

"Had," said Alar.

"What?"

"Had. We *had* all the fruit we could possibly need. We don't anymore. I destroyed the greenhouses an hour ago and cut down all the trees."

"YOU DID WHAT?!"

"Destroyed them. All of them. So I suggest that you too sit down and hear what Mistress Ashwillow has to say, because no matter how clever you think you are, I guarantee you'll not be able to rebuild before winter comes."

Lord Feffle glared at Alar like he wanted to set him on fire, not that Mistress Hearthcrow gave a damn about any of that. "And who's going to head up this council?" she said airily. "You, Glunda?"

"No," said Glunda, "because not only will its leader be a non-magic user, but I, as a former Guardian of the Golden Key will not be allowed to seek election. No former Guardian will. We had our chance and we blew it. It's time to give someone else a try."

Either side of the hall, witches and mages leapt to their feet, outraged to find themselves suddenly sidelined... for the most part at least. Some of them looked relieved they wouldn't have to worry about all that 'running stuff' non-sense anymore, and more than a few (mostly the younger ones) were quite calm and collected, like this was not news to them but was in fact what they had expected all along.

Clem Miggins laughed to see it all happen. His son frowned down at him. "I dunno what you're laughing at. You won't be on the council neither. None of you old codgers will. Like Glunda said, you had your chance and you blew it. It's time for us lot to have a go."

"Exactly," said Glunda. "No one over thirty will be allowed to stand for election. The council is for those that want to make a difference, not those who are only interested in safeguarding their tiny little piece of the pie."

Now the whole audience was on its feet, the elder members yelling their outrage until they realised that the younger members around them — of which there was significantly more — were cheering wildly. Their protests drowned out by the applause, they slowly retook their seats, as even the most uneducated among them could see in what direction the winds of change were beginning to blow.

"As I'm sure some of you are starting to realise, this proposal is not new to a lot of you. In fact, we already have a number who wish to serve, should they be deemed worthy. Clum here has very kindly offered to organise the first round of elections, which leaves us with just one piece of business to take care of." Glunda reached into the pocket of her dress and pulled out a large golden key. "Alar, would you do the honours."

Alar took the key and held it between his hands, his palms flat. He said some words and the key began to glow, the metal turning white hot as it sizzled the very air around it. Releasing his hands, the key dropped to the floor, hitting the stage with a heavy molten splat. Parts of the stage caught fire as the smell of burnt tradition permeated the silent and astonished room.

Leaving the stage, Glunda and Alar walked calmly together out the back door. On stage, Clum went over and stamped out the small fire. "Right," he said, "let's get to that vote then, shall we?"

❦❦❦❦❦

Market Square was surprisingly quiet that night, probably because most of the people were inside shouting at each other.

"Think it'll work?" said Alar.

"I've no idea," said Glunda. "But when what you were doing before doesn't work all you can do is try something else."

"I suppose," said the mage, shoving his hands in his pockets.

Glunda shrugged. "I'm sure people will hate it. People usually find a way to hate everything. But I'm guessing that so long as nobody walks away entirely happy then they're probably doing the right thing for everybody, or something like that."

Alar chuckled. "Is that some witch wisdom I've never heard of?"

"No," said Glunda, gazing up at the full moon. "Just something my dad used to say."

The End

Dexter & Sinister
DETECTING AGENTS

JOHN SINISTER IS NOT HAVING
A GOOD WEEK

Hired to look into some shady goings on
at the airship factory, his investigation
has barely begun before people start dying.
Soon he's on the wrong side of some fairly
unpleasant people, and that's before
he meets Dexter, the world's only walking,
talking, mechanical cat. That's when
things get complicated.

The Dragonfly Delivery Company

PIRATES RULE THE SKIES,
ROBBING SHIPS AT WILL

There's a rat in the Air Courier's Guild,
and to catch a rat you need a rat catcher.
You need Dexter and Sinister.

Up in the air and out of their depth,
John and Dexter will have to watch
their backs on this one. The Guild might be
on their side but the captains sure aren't.
They have secrets to keep, secrets that
could get a man killed, and it's a long way
down for those who stick their noses in
where they don't belong. And their
cats too, if they're not careful!

Dear Reader

I hope you have enjoyed reading Glunda The Veg Witch. If you are able to leave a review for Glunda somewhere it would be much appreciated. The more reviews I get the more likely I will be able to bring you tales like this in the future.

As a special thank you, please enjoy this recipe for Glunda's Bendy Veg Soup. It's sure to warm your cockles on a cold winter's night.

GLUNDA'S BENDY VEG SOUP

Ingredients:

½ a cup of red lentils (or whatever lentils you have)
a thumb sized piece of ginger, finely chopped (approx. 2 inches)
1 clove of garlic, crushed (optional)
1 tsp ground cumin
1 tsp ground coriander
½ tsp ground turmeric
a pinch of dried chilli flakes (ground chilli works just as well)
1 ½ tsp tomato puree
¼ tsp of salt
the juice from half a lemon
some olive oil
2-3 cups of bendy veg

1. Wash lentils in cold water until the water runs mostly clear.

2. Put the lentils in a medium saucepan, fill half way with boiling water, and simmer for 20 minutes until soft.

3. Whilst the lentils cook, chop the vegetables. Root vegetables
go into a bowl, to go straight in the pan. Other vegetables,
like tomato and bell pepper, will need to be fried first. As you can
use any veg in this recipe you'll have to use your discretion.
If in doubt, give them a quick fry.

Suggested vegetables:

1 cup of broccoli, diced
1 cup of potatoes, diced
½ a bell pepper or 2 tomatoes, diced
¼ cup of peas (frosted by the winter snow is fine)

4. Wash all your veg. Without peeling, remove the eyes
from the potatoes and chop into small pieces. Roughly chop
the broccoli. Set aside, along with the peas.

5. Chop the tomato/bell pepper. Set aside. Scrape the skin off
the ginger and finely chop. Skin and crush the garlic if using.

6. Heat some oil in a frying pan over a medium heat. Fry
tomato/bell pepper until soft. Add the ginger and garlic.
Fry for another thirty seconds, being careful not to let it burn.
Add the spice and fry for another thirty seconds (you may
need to add a little oil at this point). Take frying pan off the heat.

7. Once the lentils are cooked add the contents of frying pan,
using a little boiling water to swill out the frying pan. Add
remaining vegetables and top off the water until everything
is well covered.

8. Add tomato puree. Bring to the boil and simmer for
20-30 minutes on a low heat, stirring occasionally.
Once the vegetables are cooked it's ready to eat, but
the longer you can let it simmer the better, so that
the vegetables break down and the soup gets nice and thick.

9. Add salt and lemon to taste, and enjoy.

About The Author

Born a stone's throw from the Lake District, Keith studied film making at university before moving to London to work in film and TV. After twenty years of doing other people's bidding he went around the world, trained as a yoga teacher, rode a camel, got a tattoo he doesn't regret, and was finally able to publish his first novel, DEXTER & SINISTER: DE-TECTING AGENTS, something he has dreamed of since he was eight years old and asked for a typewriter for Christmas.

Currently residing in Leeds, when he's not up a mountain Keith can be found trying to get his foot behind his head. He hasn't managed it yet, but he'll get there one day.

www.keithwdickinson.com

ACKNOWLEDGEMENTS

My thanks go to Laura Bennett and Matt Wainwright, for taking the time to read Glunda and to offer their feedback and encouragement. And a special thanks to my editor, Jess Lawrence, whose experience and comprehensive knowledge of punctuation has been invaluable to me as always. If there are any mistakes in Glunda they are mine and mine alone.

Thanks also to Luisa Galstyan for a wonderful cover, and to Jen C. Mars for her excellent Glunda illustration. It was a pleasure working with you both.

www.jesslawrence.co.uk
www.fiverr.com/freelancers/luisagalstyan
www.jencmars.com